"There is no doubt in my mind that Mr. Meikle is one of the premier storytellers of our time." – Famous Monsters of Filmland

"Meikle can grace the page with words of beauty whilst twisting a nightmare into grotesque shapes before your eyes." – Len Maynard and Mick Sims, author of *The Secret Geography of Nightmare* and *Incantations*

"William Meikle's short stories and novels are shining examples of what is missing in horror fiction today: atmospheric in style, old-school in character, with an intriguing story to be told. Utmost use is made of the author's native Scotland in many of his tales, and his forays into the Cthulhu Mythos stories are original in concept, building on Lovecraft's works." – David Wynn, Mythos Books

"The best purveyor of out and out genre fiction currently plying their trade." – Dark Musings

"Part Sherlock Holmes, part Lovecraft, and all Meikle, these tales are perfect for curling up on a foggy night with a bottle and a fire." – Scott Nicholson

CARNACKI
The Edinburgh Townhouse
and Other Stories

by

William Meikle

Lovecraft ezine press

Copyright William Meikle 2017

Front Cover by Wayne Miller

Graphic Design by Kenneth W. Cain

Published by Lovecraft eZine Press

Formatting by Kenneth W. Cain

All rights reserved.

This book is licensed for your personal use only. No part of this book may be re-sold, given away, lent or reproduced to other parties by any means. Reviewers may quote small excerpts for their purposes without expressed permission by the author. If you would like to share this book with others, please consider purchasing or gifting additional copies. If you're reading this book and did not obtain it by legal means, please consider supporting the author by purchasing a copy for yourself. The author appreciates your effort to support their endeavors.

Table of Contents

The Photographer's Friend 1

Fins in the Fog 17

The Cheyne Walk Infestation 31

An Unexpected Delivery 51

A Sticky Wicket 69

The King's Treasure 85

Mr. Churchill's Surprise 105

The Edinburgh Townhouse 123

A Night in the Storeroom 153

Into the Light 173

The Photographer's Friend

I arrived on Carnacki's doorstep prompt at seven as requested. A thin layer of early frost covered the cobbled street outside 472 Cheyne Walk and I could see from the footprints leading to the door that some, if not all, of our dining club were already present.

When our host showed me in and took my overcoat I saw that I was indeed the last to arrive, and after warming my hands at the roaring fire, I joined the others in a quick snifter of brandy. Carnacki called us through to the dining room where he had taken the weather into account and provided us with thick potato soup and a most welcome hearty mutton stew that stuck to the ribs nicely and left a warm glow inside.

When we retired to the parlor it was to find that Carnacki already had another fire going in the grate and we were quite replete, warm and toasty as we filled our drinks, got smokes lit and settled down to hear the latest of our friend's adventures. He did not keep us waiting, and started as soon as we all fell quiet.

★

"This tale starts, like many others have in recent years, with a knock on my door here in Cheyne Walk. It was only this past Saturday, so the story is still fresh in my mind, although I will admit to having some qualms about relating it tonight, as it is of a somewhat upsetting nature and not one for the fainthearted. But you chaps have followed me into some dark places while sitting around the fire here, so I will ask your indulgence in following me into another. But I must warn you, where I will lead you tonight is possibly darker than any other place I have ever taken you.

"And with that caution out of the way, let us proceed, or rather, regress, to the knock on my door last Saturday.

"It was late morning, not quite noon, and I had been spending the last several hours in the library perusing a pamphlet I had procured that purported to be a summoning spell for a minor demon. It was nothing of the kind of course, although it did give me some insight into a possible new way to access the outer Macrocosm. But more of that later. It is time I stopped this rambling and got this story properly underway.

"I answered the door to find a short, portly gentleman on the step. Well, I say gentleman, but his clothes were rather shabby. He wore a baggy dark wool suit that was frayed at cuffs and ankles, and his hat had seen its best days back before the old Queen died. His forlorn-looking state might have had something to do with the rain that had left drops hanging from the brim of the aforesaid hat. More moisture hung from the poor chap's nose and wispy, ginger and spice beard. He looked up at me and for a second I wondered if he might not be about to burst into tears. He was about as miserable as any chap I have ever seen.

"Of course, I could not leave him there on the doorstep like that, so I invited him into the hallway even before asking after his business with me. At least he did not look like an itinerant salesman, and I was somewhat relieved when he turned out to be someone in rather dire need of the peculiar kind of help that I can offer."

★

"'I got your name from my doctor in Kingston, Mr. Carnacki, sir,' he said. His accent was local, with a touch of the East End to it rather than the more refined tones one might expect of a Kingstonian. But I remembered the doctor well enough when he told me the name, having helped him out a few years past with some unwanted guests in his cellar.

"I showed the portly newcomer to the library, where I got some hot tea in him. He turned down my offer of liquor, pleading a dodgy constitution and an intolerance to alcohol, and that being so I was already feeling sorry for the poor chap even before I heard his story.

"'I'm at my wit's end,' he continued once we were settled by the fire. 'If this goes on much longer I shall have to close the studio, and then where will I be? Out on the streets cap in hand I should think.'

"Once again I got the impression that he was on the verge of tears; either that or bally close to some kind of nervous breakdown.

"'Studio?' I asked, hoping to tease information from the chap without asking too many direct questions that might exacerbate what was clearly a fragile mental state.

"He nodded, and handed me a card. 'Mr. James Stenson, Photographer to the gentry' it said, and gave an address on Kingston High Street that I guessed from my knowledge of the area must be on the riverside.

"'It's my portraits, Mr. Carnacki. They're what keep the business going. Folks will pay good money these days for well taken photographs of their family, or even of their pets. That's what keeps the cash coming in and keeps the wolves from the door. But for the past two weeks I haven't been able to get a single one to develop without the blasted thing appearing in them.'

"I did not even have to ask after the manner of said 'blasted thing', for Stenson had brought something that is considerably rare in my line of work; he had brought tangible evidence. What it was evidence of, I had no idea, but he took a set of twelve portrait photographs from his wallet and handed them to me, one by one, without comment.

"A variety of people and social classes were on display, some in fine expensive clothes, others in more workmanlike garb, and there was even a man with a huge bull mastiff that I took to be one of the aforesaid pets.

"But there was one common factor in every one, a bloated, gray form, almost the size of a soccer ball and hunched like a squat curmudgeonly toad, which was there in every photograph, perched on a sitters' left shoulder. It had a rudimentary face that was little more than button eyes, a slit for a mouth and two tiny holes for nostrils, but the expression was obvious. It grinned, or rather, it leered, into the camera. It looked exactly as one would imagine it would if it were taunting the photographer."

★

"'They're all like that, sir' Stenson said when I handed the photographs back to him. 'Not only in this lot either. Everybody that has sat for me these past two weeks has that thing on their shoulder. At first I thought it was perhaps a bad spot on my lens, but I've swapped them around several times and I still get the same result. Besides, what manner of bally flaw on a lens would sit there and smile like that? I've been in this business for some years now, and I know my onions, so to speak. Despite that, I haven't a single clue what is going on here.'

"'And it's not a problem in the development?' I asked. 'Some fault with the composition of the chemicals, or your enlargement process perhaps?'

"He shook his head, then, with a pained expression, rubbed at his stomach as if trying to calm a possible eruption.

"'Sorry, sir,' he said when he saw I had taken note. 'It's this blasted nuisance. It's got my nerves in a mess and my internals all at sixes and sevens so I don't know which way I'm going. And I have indeed ruled out anything untoward in the process. I've changed every single piece of equipment in the studio out for new kit. I've even slung out a whole batch of the chemicals that cost me a pretty penny I won't see again. The results are always the same. The blasted thing keeps appearing, and keeps staring straight at me.'

"He tapped at the top photograph. It showed a severe, bewhiskered, military gent in full uniform that was rather too tight for him. The toad-like thing was there, leering, almost a grin. It was semi-translucent, but the chap was right, there was no way it could be mistaken for a problem with the lens or processing. It was too real, and obviously present for that to be the case.

"I filled a pipe and passed the tobacco pouch over to Stenson, taking the time it took him to get a pipe lit to ponder the situation. Of course, my first thought was that it must be some kind of prank, or perhaps even Stenson's own doing, looking to make some money from lurid exploitation of so-called 'spirit photography'. But, dash it if the fellow did not look so forlorn, so bally lost and needy. If he was acting, he was making a bloody good show of it.

"By the time he had got his pipe lit to his satisfaction I had made my decision. I went with my gut feeling and decided to trust him. That still did not, of course, rule out the possibility that it was a prank, possibly one being undertaken by a business competitor of Stenson's or someone with an axe to grind. But Stenson pleaded ignorance when I asked if he had made any enemies in the recent past.

"'I don't know who would take that kind of umbrage,' he said. 'Would I hurt a fly? I only want to take my pictures. That's all I've ever wanted.'

"'And there was nothing untoward in the days before the first appearance of your nuisance?'

"He shook his head.

"'I've been wracking my brains these past weeks trying to think on it, Mr. Carnacki. I keep coming up blank.'

"'Well, I suggest that you wrack them a little harder, old chap,' I replied. 'But in the meantime, we had better get down to your studio and see what's what.'"

★

"We took a carriage down the north side of the river to Kingston. In other circumstances I might have taken the train, but given the nature of the thing that perched in all the photographs, I thought it prudent to travel with my box of defenses, just in case. It was far simpler just to call for a carriage than to lug the box around from pillar to post.

I paid for the journey, and Stenson was most relieved that I had done so, although he put up a token resistance at first as we left Chelsea behind heading west. I insisted, and then, after thanking me for my generosity, he explained his circumstances.

"'I am afraid that you find me in rather dire straits. I am properly strapped, Mr. Carnacki,' he said. 'I can generally live from fortnight to fortnight, so two weeks without cash will about do me in. The rent's due next week, and there's no money to pay for it if you can't help me out here with the nuisance. Even then, I shall have to get all the sitters from the last two weeks back in for another shoot. That's another headache I am not looking forward to, I'll tell you that for nothing.'

"Yet again, I thought the poor chap looked to be on the verge of tears, and he rubbed at his belly, kneading it like a baker working dough, before grimacing as if in pain.

"'Let's take things one problem at a time, shall we?' I said. 'Pass me those photographs again.'

"He did as I asked, and I took the photographs from him. I shuffled though them, proceeding more slowly on this occasion, looking to see if I had missed anything of import on my first perusal. Now that I took a closer look, I saw that the toad-thing wasn't quite identical in all the portraits. It appeared to be more substantial in some than in others, and I could not see a pattern in it, until a thought struck me.

"I checked the back of the photographs, and found that my hunch had been right. Stenson had put a name and a date stamp on each in black ink. I quickly rearranged them into chronological order and had another look at the images. Now that I knew what I was looking for it was obvious; the bally thing was becoming more and more real, more solid, in each successive image.

"'When was the last one of these taken?' I asked, although I already knew, having read the date stamp mere seconds before.

"'Yesterday morning,' the man replied. 'I closed the studio for the day today and have not taken any since that one in your hand.'

"I knew then what my first action would be on reaching Kingston. I was going to sit for a photograph for him. Then we would see what we would see."

★

"I had been correct in my surmise about his address being on the river, but after he helped me unload my box from the carriage and carry it to his premises, I quickly discovered that Stenson may have somewhat overstated the commercial nature of his business. His studio was rather less grand than the word suggests, being little more than a large room above a tailor's premises in the High Street. It did have the advantage of facing south over the river, and it had two large bay windows that let in plenty of light.

"His development room was likewise rather rudimentary, being merely a modified closet to the rear. But everything was clean and tidy and I could tell he took no little pride in his work, given the manner in which he gave me the tour of his domain. I did notice, however, that he took pains to skirt around the large wing backed chair he obviously used for his sitters. It was the same chair I had seen in all the photographs that he had shown me so far.

"As I have said, the premises were rather rudimentary. The tour took no more than three or four minutes before it brought us back to the entrance where we came in. We had left my box of defenses by the main door and as yet I could see no need for them, for this manifestation, whatever it was, showed no sign of being any danger beyond its habit of messing up perfectly good photographs. And at least I knew that my materials would be available at short notice should the circles, or even the pentacle, be required.

"Stenson had relaxed somewhat, now that he was back in familiar, if not exactly comfortable, surroundings, but it was clear he was now waiting for me to fulfil my end of our little bargain

"At first, when I told him of my plan to sit for a photograph and see what came out in the development, he would not hear of it. He spluttered and pleaded a fear for my safety, but I could tell it was fear of what he might see in the final photograph that gave him pause. I insisted that he proceed, and that I took full responsibility for my own wellbeing and, after some gentle persuasion on my part in which I played to his professional pride, he finally relented.

"He had me sit in the high backed chair in front of a dark velvet curtain that was draped across the wall opposite the windows. Of course I checked behind the drapes first before I sat down; I was still not completely persuaded that this was all not some manner of hoax. But there was only bare wall behind the cloth. I rapped on the plaster but all I did was dislodge some loose patches. There were no obvious hollows, and if it was a trick, it was one beyond my comprehension.

"After he got me seated, Stenson hummed and hawed over the light, the angle of the shot and the overall composition with such a fuss that finally I had to raise my voice and tell him to get on with it. Even then it took an interminable time for him to be satisfied enough to take a shot of me.

"But finally, thankfully, it was done. He took the bally picture, the flash momentarily blinded me and left me with dancing yellow patches in my eyes for long seconds afterward. Then Stenson locked himself away in the developing room for what seemed like hours.

"I left the chair and stood by the larger of the two bay windows. I smoked several cigarettes, watching the world go by in Kingston High Street below me as the afternoon wore on and the light went from the sky. At one point I thought I heard an exclamation from within the small room, then a noise that sounded like Stenson might be retching, but when I shouted through the door, he assured me that everything was fine. His voice sounded weak and tired, but I did not breach the darkness of the developing room, for I knew I would ruin the work in progress should I do so.

"Finally Stenson returned. His face was pale, his eyes wide, and I knew, even before he showed me, what I would see on the photograph. I took the still glistening sheet from his trembling hand as he went back to kneading his ample belly.

"He took a dashed good picture, I will give him that, for I looked quite handsome, even if I do say so myself. Or rather, I would have looked handsome, had it not been for the squat, gray, toad-like thing that sat, smirking, on my left shoulder."

★

"Now, I know you chaps will believe me when I say that I had felt nothing on that shoulder while sitting for the photograph, and you know from my tales that I have developed a certain sensitivity to such things. There had been no cold spot, no sense of any contact with the beyond, no weight or smell or touch. There had been nothing whatsoever to suggest I was not the only object in the frame.

"And yet, that toad-thing had been there. It was in the blasted photograph, larger than life, and it was even more solid seeming now than in any of the images I had perused in the carriage. I was at a complete loss to explain it, and Stenson was working up into quite a state over the matter again.

"We retired to a local hostelry down the street where a pint of ale for me, a large mug of sweet tea for him, and some pie and mash did much to calm him down, although he left more than half of the meal on his plate, pleading intestinal discomfort. For my own part, I polished mine off in short order to fortify me for what I knew needed doing that same night.

"'Well, now you've seen it for yourself, Mr. Carnacki,' he said. 'And now you know it's not some kind of a trick. Can you help me? Please say you can help me?'

"'I am confident I can,' I said, and at the time I said it, I jolly well meant it, for I had my skills, my knowledge, and my defenses. All I needed was some time alone in the vicinity of the phenomenon.

"I sent Stenson away. He lived in a small terraced house several streets to the north, and I instructed him, in no uncertain terms, to stay at home until the morning. I warned him of dire consequences should he interrupt me in my work. Of course, I did not believe any such thing, but I did need some peace and quiet for what I needed to be about that night. After watching him walk away, I returned to the upstairs studio, and begin to make my preparations."

★

Carnacki paused at this juncture to refill his pipe. As if as an afterthought, he reached into his jacket pocket and brought out a photograph that he passed firstly to me, as I was the man in the chair immediately to his left. It was the same photograph that he had described being taken.

He was right, the man Stenson did have an eye for a good composition, and Carnacki did indeed look resplendent and confident in the image. But that was only the second thing I noticed.

The squat gray toad caught my gaze and would not let me look away. Carnacki had also been quite right in his description. It sat smirking, on his shoulder like some devilish idol. And despite its smile, I took a sudden chill on seeing it, one that ran all the way up my spine.

I passed the damned thing on to Jessop and headed for a fresh drink, making it a double for I was suddenly in quite a funk. I gulped a full half of it down before turning back toward my chair, and I only arrived back in my seat in time to see Carnacki put the photograph away in his pocket, light his pipe, and continue.

★

"So now you chaps know exactly the manner of thing that I was up against. If it was indeed some kind of manifestation from the Great Beyond, it was a dashed queer one and outside my realm of experience. But if it was really there, I was pretty sure I would be able to make it show itself via the use of the pentacle and my color theory.

"I wasted no time on arriving back in the studio in setting up the circles and the pentacle, and as it was turning full dark I was ready to begin.

"I was, to tell the truth, more excited than anything else, for I saw this as an opportunity to test the box of switches and knobs that I had been working on. This little new piece of kit will, when properly finished, finally allow me to modulate and control the brightness of the colors of the valves, and also set them to a pulsing frequency that I can also modulate depending on the required circumstances. In future it will, I am sure, stand me in good stead in dark places.

"But that night in the studio, I did not get much of a chance to use its full capabilities. I sat inside the pentacle on top of the empty box that carried my defenses, smoking my pipe and waiting for the toad to make its appearance. But there was nothing in the room except shifting shadows.

"The valves stayed steady, with no hint of any presence for them to defend against, and the room was so quiet I heard my own heart thud in my chest. After a few hours of this, I got rather fed up with waiting. I took to playing with the aforesaid box of tricks, experimenting to see if different options of color and frequency of pulses might bring the toad into the visible spectrum.

"I put the pentacle through a wide variety of combinations of color washes and pulsation, but to no avail. All I succeeded in doing was making the shadowy areas of the room a bit more colorful, which was dashed pretty, but of little use in solving Stenson's predicament.

"In the end I gave up, and smoked another pipe, but there was still no sign of any apparition, and my boredom wasn't far from the surface. I could not find any calmness that would allow me to settle. Taking things into my own hands, I left the pentacle running and stepped out of the circle, being careful not to disturb the protections.

"I stood still outside the defenses, chewing on the stem on my pipe and ready to step back into safety at a moment's notice.

"But still nothing happened."

★

"I gave up the vigil in the pentacle as a bad lot, but I was not yet finished experimenting for the night. I turned up the valves to their fullest extent and took to Stenson's cameras for the next stage.

"I took a series of photographs of the pentacle, of myself inside it, and of the shadows in the corners, hoping that the toad thing would be seen in at least one of them, and give me a starting point from which to search for it.

"By the time I had developed the photographs, it was well into the depths of the night. At least I got a nice set of pictures out of it that I will be keeping with the notes of the case. But apart from that they only showed what I had seen for myself. There was merely an empty room and the pentacle on the floor with dark shadows in the corners.

"I was at a loss, for the time being, as to what else I could do.

"I stepped back into the pentacle and sat there, with the valves dimmed to their lowest ebb to conserve the battery, and waited to see what might occur, but in my heart I already knew the night was a lost cause.

"For all my vaunted expertise and knowledge, I was no

closer to helping Stenson than I had been when he turned up on my doorstep."

★

"At some point I fell asleep, sitting upright on the box, and I must have been that way for some hours, for I had a bally stiff back and neck when I finally woke. Thin morning sunlight was coming in through the bay windows, and there was still neither hide nor hair of my quarry.

"I knew that Stenson would be along shortly, expecting a report, perhaps even hoping for a conclusion. I made a tour of the whole studio, inspecting everything, even the inside of the cameras themselves, looking behind every drape, into every bottle and jar in the development room. I rapped on walls and floorboards looking for hidden closets or chambers, and I even jumped up and down on the floorboards, looking for any that might be concealing a secret swivel. I am afraid I must have cut a jolly frustrated figure by the time Stenson arrived just after eight a.m.

"He must have seen it in my face, for he did not immediately broach the subject, but instead invited me to the hostelry along the road for breakfast. I left the pentacle laid out on the floor, in case I might return to it later.

"The hostelry was quiet, it being so early of a Sunday morning and we took a table with a view looking out over the river. This time Stenson insisted on paying, although I noted he only partook of a small pot of tea. I however fortified myself with bacon, eggs and a mound of toast, and was feeling slightly better about the situation by the time I sat back and lit a smoke. It was only then that we spoke of the frustrations of my long dark vigil.

"'And there is nothing untoward in any of the photographs that you took?' the stocky man said.

"I shook my head.

"'Then perhaps your magic circle did the trick after all? Perhaps it has merely moved off somewhere else?'

"I shook my head again,

"'It is my experience that such things do not merely move on unbidden. They are generally here for a reason. And I am not done yet. There is one more experiment that is yet required, and it is one that I could not undertake with without your presence.'

"'And what is that, Mr. Carnacki?'

"'We need to go back to the studio. You must sit for a photograph yourself. We must see what that shows us.'"

★

"Once again he spluttered, prevaricated and rubbed hard at the flesh of his belly as if trying to keep something inside him from moving around.

"'I am not sure I like that idea, Mr. Carnacki,' he said.

"'And I am not sure we have any choice in the matter,' I replied. 'You asked me here for my advice? Well there it is. You may take it or leave it as you choose.'

"I saw him fight with the fear behind his eyes and decided to give him a nudge in the right direction.

"'When did you say your rent was due?' I said.

"That finally got him moving. But I could sense the apprehension in the poor chap as we made our way back to the studio. He walked slowly, as if every step was onerous, and when we got to the door, he turned to me, his face ashen.

"'Do you really think this is absolutely necessary?'

"I had to bodily push him inside and stand to block his way back out so that his only option was to go up the stairs. I reminded him of what I'd said back in the hotel only minutes previously.

"'You asked for my help, old man,' I replied. 'I am giving it to you, the only way I know how. But if you'd rather, I can pick up my box of tricks and be on my way…'

"At that, he relented, and we made our way up to the studio.

"Even then, I had a dashed hard job to get him to sit in the armchair in front of the drapes. I thought for a time he was in too much of a funk for any attempt at a photograph to be made. But when I reminded him again of his stricken finances, and the looming deadline of his rent payment, he finally saw sense and sat still long enough for me to continue with the preparations.

"He did, however, keep up a constant chatter of advice as I set up his camera and flash, and I could see that he was nervous about letting anyone else use the equipment. I had to insist.

"'Sit still, please, Mr. Stenson,' I said softly. 'This is the only way we are going to get to the bottom of this matter.'

"Finally, we were both ready, and I was able to take the photograph. I watched closely. From my point of view, there was no sign of any intruding presence on his shoulder.

"After the photograph was taken, Stenson headed for the development room, and all I could do was smoke my pipe, stare out at the Sunday strollers braving the elements on the riverside walk, and wait."

★

"When he finally emerged, he was more ashen than ever and looked positively ill. Once again I took a newly developed photograph from a trembling hand.

"The toad like thing was there again, but it wasn't on his shoulder. It sat in his lap, snuggled tight against his ample belly. The squat head was turned toward the camera and the smile, which was now wide-mouthed and full of tiny teeth, did not look humorous at all. It looked positively malignant.

"'What does this mean, Mr. Carnacki?' Stenson said.

"'It means that it is not your studio or your equipment that is the focus of this manifestation, Mr. Stenson,' I replied, suddenly sure I was speaking the truth. I stepped over to my circles and switched on the pentacle. 'It is bound to you, attached to your very person. That is the reason it did not show up when you were not present in the room. Quickly now, into the pentacle. We must see if the properties of my defenses will facilitate a cleansing.'

"Again I had to bodily manhandle him to go where he needed to go. I went over, took him by the right arm, and marched him to the circles.

"'Step in,' I said. 'But do not touch the lines.'

"He was reluctant, and just then a spasm hit him, hard, almost doubling him over. I saw pain etched on his face.

"'Quickly,' I said. I stepped into the pentacle and tried

to get him to join me inside the defenses, but he would not step forward.

"'It hurts. It hurts too much,' he wailed, and another spasm of pain hit him. He bent double, stumbled, and almost fell. His left foot dragged across both the inner and outer circles and in doing so, knocked over the green valve. It smashed into fine shards on the floor, and with a crack and a spark my pentacle went dim and quiet."

★

"After that Stenson would have nothing to do with me. Indeed it appeared he fully intended to blame me, my pentacle and the defensive circles for his spasms of pain. I cleaned up and packed away my kit into the box in the face of a moody, almost sullen silence that emanated off him in waves.

"I tried, several times, to impress upon him the seriousness of the thing that had obviously attached itself to him, but he brushed me away.

"'I have an apprentice, and he can take the pictures for the business,' he said. 'I do not even have to be present here at all. So, you see, Mr. Carnacki, you have indeed solved my problem for me.'

"He ushered me out the door as if he was glad to see the back of me, so I did not get a chance to explain to him what I knew of death omens, and harbingers, and what I suspected his companion to be.

"I do not believe it would have done him much good in any case, for I think he now considered me a crackpot at best and a charlatan at worst, and I would not be given a chance to redeem myself of either charge."

★

Carnacki stopped, and it was with some surprise that we realized his tale was done.

Arkwright was almost apoplectic.

"Damn it, man, you can't leave it like that. What the blazes happened next?"

Carnacki sighed, and I saw deep sadness in his eyes.

"I failed the man," Carnacki replied softly. "I should have insisted that he stand inside the pentacle; perhaps even at the threat of violence. I might then be up on an assault case in the court, but at least he might still be alive to press charges."

"You mean the photographer died?" Arkwright said in a whisper.

Carnacki nodded and took a long gulp to finish off his drink.

"Two days ago. His apprentice found him in the studio. I inquired discretely with his doctor as to the cause; he was the man who recommended me to Stenson in the first place. It appears that Stenson's internal organs all gave way. The doctor said it was as if something had eaten him hollow from the inside, although he had no earthly idea as to what might have done it so rapidly."

We were all infused with some of Carnacki's sadness, and we left in silence, lost in our own thoughts as he showed us to the door.

"Now, out you go," he said.

FINS IN THE FOG

I made my way to Chelsea full of anticipation of a new, lively adventure to make up for what had, quite frankly, been a terribly depressing week at the workplace. But my concerns for my own state of mind were quickly dispelled when my friend opened the door to my knock.

Carnacki looked pale and wan, one might almost say sickly. He waved away my protestations, and led me through to the library where the chaps were gathered having a smoke and a glass of sherry. Carnacki was unusually quiet at first, although it would have been difficult for him to speak in any case, as Arkwright was expounding at some length on the disgraceful conditions prevalent during his daily commute in the Tube system.

Once we went to table, a fine meal of a delicious vegetable soup, and a main course of venison and potatoes washed down with some strong London Porter did much to put some color in Carnacki's cheeks. By the time we retired to his parlor, charged our glasses and got fresh smokes lit, he seemed more than keen to proceed with the latest of his adventures.

We quickly settled into the story, his soft tones talking us swiftly away to another night, a fog-filled evening, and a rap at the same door we had all come in through an hour or so earlier.

★

"You have all heard me speak of Captain Gault before," Carnacki began. "The old ruffian and I have shared, and crossed swords, on several cases together now. I hesitate to call him a pirate, but it is a designation that fits him as well as any other, although for the most part our meetings have been amicable.

"The time we have spent in each other's company has been more than enough for us to get the measure of each other's mettle. I know him to be a bluff cove, and not above a bit of criminality should there be a sniff of a profit in it. But I did not expect to have him at my door near midnight of a November night.

"Indeed, at first I didn't recognize the disheveled figure that crouched like a whipped cur on the doorstep when I answered the knock. It was only when he spoke that I knew my man, although his voice held a hint of something I had never heard in it before; it sounded like fear or, more accurately, terror.

"'You must help me, Carnacki. Only you can help me.'"

★

"Even before I could welcome him in, he had pushed passed me into the hallway.

"'Let me in, man,' he implored me. 'Quickly now, before it catches the scent again.'

"Of course, I could not then close the door without checking to see what he thought might be after him. But on looking out, both ways along the street, I saw only a thin late autumnal fog rolling up from the Embankment. That was nothing unusual for the season, but as soon as he saw the fog, Gault grew even more agitated than he already had been.

"'Get in, man. Now, if you value your life!'

"There was such an urgency in his tone that I decided it might be prudent to trust him on the matter, at least until I had got to the bottom of the reason for his sudden arrival. I acquiesced and shut us inside against the night air.

"That small act did much to calm my visitor, and he allowed me to lead him through to the library where I had been sitting reading by the fire. He still did not fully relax, despite several stiff measures of my best Scotch and a pipe of my strong Egyptian blend of tobacco. He also flatly refused to take off the voluminous overcoat in which he was wrapped, even while sitting in front of the full warmth of my fire.

"'I really do mean to tell you my tale, Carnacki,' he said

after a time. He had some color in his cheeks now, but there was still an evident strain around his eyes and lips as he continued. 'But it is a long and an outlandish story, even by our standards, and I think a demonstration might quicker serve my purposes in the matter. But I cannot risk taking you out into the street. Have you any access to your roof from here inside?'

"It was a strange request, but I could see that the man was still a bundle of nerves, and it was a terrible thing to see in a chap I might even consider thinking of as a friend. I resolved there and then to do anything I could to ease his state of mind.

"We took fresh drinks with us. I led him up to my attic staircase and we clambered up and out of the window onto the flat narrow ledge below the main chimney. It was quite warm here despite the chill November air, the old brickwork being heated by my fires below, but still Gault huddled inside his overcoat.

"He stepped forward, rather precariously to my mind, and went to the roof's edge to look down at the street. He motioned that I should move alongside him as he pointed downward.

"'Come and see. Trust me, it will be in the damned fog. It's always in the damned fog. It's after me, Carnacki. It has been after me all the way from the bloody Carib, and I do not know how to escape it.'

"I eased forward gingerly to join him at the edge of the roof, and looked down. At first all I saw was the aforesaid fog. It was thicker now, and turgid, flowing almost like water up from the river and filling the whole breadth of the street below to the depth of several feet. Then I felt something, a tingling vibration, like a warning of approaching thunder, and the hairs on the back of my hands stood on end as static built in the air.

"'It's here,' Gault said, almost a moan, and pointed down toward the end of the street where it met the Embankment. 'The damnable thing has found me again.'

"I followed his indication and looked that way. The fog was being raised slightly, a v-shaped wave travelling through it as something approached from the river, as if something large swam under the surface. Whatever the bally thing was, it was long and smooth, exuding an air of both menace and implacability as it came, impossibly, up the street.

"It showed its true nature seconds later. A tall triangular dorsal fin, as high as the length of my leg from hip to toe broke the surface layer. The fog was too thick to allow the sight of much else, but that high, gray, almost translucent fin, cruising majestically up a London street through the fog, was enough to convince me that Gault was indeed in definite trouble.

"We stood there for long seconds in silence. I had no words to say, struck dumb as I was by the sheer impossibility of the view below. The thing must have been a good twenty feet from nose to tail. I believe that 'shark' is the best word for it, although it is too small a word for the enormity of the thing I saw there in the street.

"We watched as it cruised for the whole length of Cheyne Walk. It headed past my door and up to the end of the road before turning on its tail and coming back down again. The sway of the fin showed that it was drifting slightly from side to side, giving every indication that it was on the hunt.

"I now understood why he had come, with all due haste, to my doorstep. He needed defending, and I might well be the only man in London capable of the task.

"After ensuring that the thing had, for the time being at least, gone past my doorway again and was headed south, away back toward the Embankment, Gault took my arm and led me back inside.

"'It is exactly what it appears to be; a bloody phantom shark. And it's after me, Carnacki. It won't stop hunting me, and it is out for blood.'"

★

"I found out exactly what he meant about blood when we went back down to sit by the fire in the library. He knocked back another large measure of my scotch before, slowly, and wincing as if it caused him some degree of pain, he eased off his captain's coat and showed me his left arm. The full length of it, from wrist to high on the shoulder was swathed in fresh, white, bandages.

"He flexed his fingers, and grimaced in pain again.

"'At least the blasted thing still works, after a fashion. But I damned near lost the arm altogether,' he said. 'I got lazy in

Dover. I thought that once I was ashore and off the boat I was away and free, out of the bloody thing's reach for good. But as you saw for yourself on the roof, this thing is not bound to the sea. No, if it is bound to anything of this earth, it is bound to me, and I must be rid of it. You must help me, Carnacki. Please, before it is the death of me?'

"I poured us both another scotch. In truth, I needed it quite as much as he, for the sight of a bally huge shark cruising up and down Cheyne Walk had quite unsettled me. I took one of his strong black Russian cigarettes when he offered, and, finally, I got his tale. It took him quite some time, and it is one that is far too long to relate to you chaps here, but I will attempt to give you the basics as he told them to me so that you might understand what comes next.

"Gault and his crew were in the Bahamas this past summer. As far as I could ascertain it was something to do with a wreck to be salvaged and a profit to be made, as is usually the case with the good captain. But the salvage operation was doomed almost before it began, as they quickly found out that sharks controlled the waters above the wreck. One large Great White in particular proved most troublesome, and made off with two of Gault's men before he did something about it.

"And that something was rather spectacular. Our captain did not have much experience with the great predators, but he knows explosives only too well. He lured the beast in with bait that masked several sticks of dynamite and blew the bally thing to bits, strewing it all across the ocean.

"It was only after the deed was done that Gault saw the three, smaller, sharks floating, dead in the bloody ruin that was left. The beast he'd blown up had been pregnant, and near full term at that.

"Very soon after that, Gault discovered that the great shark's bloody revenge was not going to be foiled by the small inconvenience of its violent death."

★

"Their salvage of the wreck proved to be at an end. Any attempt to go into the water was met by a strange fog that came up out of nowhere, accompanied by the appearance of a ghostly fin, cruising menacingly in wide, lazy, circles around the boat.

The crew took a funk, and refused to go into the water. Mutiny was close, even after Gault decided to cut his losses and run for home. They did not escape. The fog, and the spectral beast within it, followed them, all the way across the ocean, the great fin creeping ever closer to their hull with each night that passed.

"They lost a man on the fifth night. His body, or what was left of it, was found inside the main cargo bay, mutilated and torn almost beyond recognition. The hull was no longer enough to keep the shark at bay. The crewmen took to remaining wherever possible on the upper decks, for that was at least above the fog most of the time. But as the gray gloom grew ever thicker and crept higher toward the gunwales, so the shark grew ever more emboldened.

"Soon it was seen in other parts of the ship, and although the men took pains to ensure they were never alone, still the thing took them, silently, picking them off one by one, leaving only torn, bloody remains behind.

"By the time the boat reached Dover, Gault had lost eight men, and every man remaining fled ashore as soon as they docked, fleeing the fog that now enveloped the whole vessel even although the port sat under a clear, starry sky.

"Gault was not immune to the fear that had gripped the crew. He joined them in abandoning the boat, and heading to the nearest inn, hoping that drink and company might ease his torment at the loss of his men and allow him to forget, for a time at least.

"But the shark found him, as soon as he ventured out. He'd left the bar to use the courtyard privy, and the fog fell on him like a wet blanket. As he had shown me, he had escaped with his life but not before the shark had got close enough to ravage his arm.

"'It was right cold where it gripped, Carnacki,' he said in a soft voice as he remembered. 'As if I had my arm trapped between two blocks of ice. I felt the teeth pierce my flesh, felt pain like you would not believe, then it shook me from side to side, like it was playing with me. I had to shuck off my jacket to escape, then I fled. For a time the fog followed me, until I reached a hill and was able to rise out of its reach. When I looked back, it was moving away from me again, moving back towards where we'd docked the boat. I was in no mood to go back.

"'I ran for hours, heading inland, attempting to put as much distance between myself and the fog as I possibly could. But I had lost too much blood, and I was weak to the point of collapse when I was found on the road several miles from the docks.

"'They took me to a local doctor who patched me up nicely. He wanted me to stay in bed for a week, but I knew the fog, and the blasted shark wouldn't give me the time; I knew it would still be after me.

"'So I took my leave of the good doctor and I ran again. I ran for days, my only thought being that there was only one man in England who might believe me and be able to do something about it. And now I have finally made my way here.

"'But it hunts me. It hunts me still, Carnacki, and you are the only one I trust to get me out of this blasted mess.'"

★

At this point, Carnacki stopped talking, both to give us a chance to refill our glasses, and to digest the import of the story so far. But the break was a brief one, for we were all eager to know what happened next, and even Arkwright held off from his usual questions. We were soon once again seated and comfortable for the next chapter in the tale. Carnacki went on, picking up where he had left off.

★

"If I had not looked down for myself at that great fin in the fog, I might have dismissed Gault's story as the ravings of a wounded man. But I had seen it with my own eyes, and I could also note the funk and terror that gripped the captain. The normally stout and fearless man I thought I knew was scared out of his wits and that more than anything convinced me of the seriousness of our situation.

"And things grew worse quickly, for as I was refilling our glasses, I felt the strange tingling in the air again, and the rise of the hairs on the back of my hands. Gault felt it too, and he looked at me pleadingly.

"'I am done running from the blasted thing, Carnacki. It ends here, one way or the other. Can you help me?'

"'I can certainly try,' I said.

"I had him rise and move aside as I removed the rugs from the floor to uncover the defensive pentagram and circles I have inlaid in the hardwood of the floor. It was only a matter of seconds before we stepped into the circles but even so we were almost too late, for fine fog curled in below the library door and the air cracked with electricity.

"I wished I had been given time to set up my valves and electric pentacle, but the gear was stowed under the stairs and although I could see the cupboard door from where I stood, experience told me it was already too late to move out of the protections.

"The fog kept coming, thickening and swirling. It did not cross over my protective lines though, and soon we stood inside a circle of clear air while the rest of the floor of my small library was completely obscured in thick gray that was over a foot deep and thickening by the second. The sense of something approaching was almost palpable. The electricity in the air caused the hair on our heads to stand out like a mane. It would have been almost comical had we not been in such a bally blue funk.

"When the great shark finally came, it passed through the door, although I did not even have time to consider the sheer impossibility of it. One second there was only fog, and the next the tall fin was circling my protections, leaving a wake behind it that sent cold gray waves lapping against my circles, and with the fog below it shifting aside as if something of enormous bulk moved beneath the surface. That was another impossibility of course, for the fog itself was only a foot deep above the floor. But I was not thinking of that; the static in the air sent blue sparks cracking around us like lightning bolts, and I smelled ozone and sulfurous gas, thick and cloying in nostrils and throat. Gault moaned, and shrank into a cowering stance as if expecting an imminent attack.

"'Courage, man,' I said. 'The circle will hold.'

"I was no means as sure of myself as I had sounded for

his benefit, for the cracking static was battering against my defensive ring with all the ferocity of a thunderstorm. The great fin circled, faster and faster, as if sensing a weakness, ready to surge and rend and tear.

"I did the only thing I could think of at that moment. I raised my voice in a chant to add to the protections, one that had served me well in previous tight spots. As with most rituals, the words themselves did not matter, it was the rhythm of the thing, and the intent with which they were said.

"'*Ri linn dioladh na beatha Ri linn bruchdadh na falluis,*
"'*Ri linn iobar na creadha, Ri linn dortadh na fala.*'

"The response was immediate. The sparks of electricity cut off as if a switch had been thrown. The huge fin sank down into the fog until the tip of it was below the surface, then the fog itself sank away, disappearing into the floor as quickly as it had come.

"We were left in a cold, quiet, library, the only sound the cracking of damp wood in the fireplace as it burned."

★

"'You did it," Gault said, clapping me on the shoulder. "You sent the blasted thing back to hell.'

"'I sincerely doubt that's where it came from, old chap,' I replied. 'And besides, we can't count our chickens yet. I fear the night has only begun.'

"All the while I was speaking I had kept an eye on the gap below the door, looking for any recurrence of the fog. Judging that the risk was worth the reward, I stepped quickly out of the circle, heading for the under-stair cupboard. Gault made to follow me but I motioned him back.

"'Stay there. It is you that it wants, and I shall only be a few minutes. Watch the door and pay attention. If you sense its return, shout.'

"My first thought had been to set up the electric pentacle, but I was worried about the electrical aspect of this manifestation, and I had a better protection for that than the valves and wires. It took a bit of effort on my part, for the thing is dashed heavy, but I managed, eventually, to lug my Faraday cage out from the back of the cupboard, along with the larger of my two diesel generators.

"Installing the generator meant me going out into the hall, for I could not run the bally thing in the enclosed space of the library; the fumes would kill us faster than any blasted shark. I worked quickly, expecting an attack at any moment. But none came. I opened the kitchen door and the window above the sink to enable a free flow of fresh air, and set the generator going before returning to the protections. With Gault lending a hand as much as he was able to, it was only a matter of a few more minutes to get the mesh cage erected inside the circle.

"I had Gault join me inside the cube before I switched it on. We had to sit, and it was a dashed tight squeeze. In all honesty it made me feel rather foolish but the hum from the cage itself, and the thrum of the generator out in the hall were almost comforting in themselves. I also had the foresight to fetch some Scotch in with us, along with some smokes, so we did not want for distraction while we awaited the shark's next move."

★

"We sat and smoked in silence for a while.

"'Maybe you were wrong, Carnacki.' Gault said after a time. "Mayhap the thing is indeed gone.'

"'I wish that it were so, my friend," I replied. 'But in my experience, apparitions such as this take a bit more persuasion than a bit of Celtic chanting to make them take their leave.'

"My hunch was all too unfortunately proven right minutes later. I had left the main library door open as access for the generator's cables, so we were able to see thick fog creeping through the hallway before it reached the room. There was no anticipatory tingling this time; the Faraday cage was working, insofar as it blocked the rising static that marked the approach of the phenomenon. But my nerves were on edge and I had to force a tremor out of my hands as I finished a cigarette and rubbed the butt between my fingers to stub it out.

"The fog rolled into the room in waves, and all too soon we were once again adrift in a circle of clear air amid a sea of impenetrable gray. And this time it did not stop coming. Wave after wave of it, rising ever deeper, flowed in through the doorway until it was two, three, four feet deep around us.

"In less than a minute it had filled the whole room, leaving us encased inside a shimmering dome of protection. Blue sparks and jagged bolts of blinding light flew against the surface of our defenses, but inside the cage we heard nothing but a gentle hum, felt nothing but a soft, almost comforting, vibration.

"Our feeling of safety did not last long, for despite the sturdy security of the cage, it quickly became obvious we were no longer alone in the fog. Something moved, beyond the perimeter of my defensive circle, something long and sleek and implacably intent on our complete and utter destruction.

"When the attack finally came, it was swift and merciless."

★

"We saw the head first, a great flat wedge near as wide as the cage inside which we huddled. It surged forward, a huge snout loomed up out of the fog and the shark hit the outer circle with a blow that shook the whole library. Even while the defenses were still reverberating from the first hit, it came again, slightly side on this time, raising the snout so that a massive maw of a mouth filled with far too many teeth tried to take a bite out of our shield.

"I tasted salt spray at my lips, smelled rotting fish, felt too-hot breath in my face. The Faraday cage whined, as if the generator had come under a great strain, then the outer defensive circle's protection crumbled completely. Fog rushed in to fill the void and surround us completely. The only clear air at our disposal was now inside the cage itself. Beyond that our little electrical cube was adrift, lost in the sea of fog, and at the mercy of the next attack.

"I heard a groan and turned, alarmed to see that Gault was slumped down at my side, grasping his bad arm. His face was ashen, and red blotches showed through the white of the bandages; he had taken a knock, probably during that first, hammer-like blow of the snout.

"I had hoped that we might be able to wait this thing out, hoping that the defenses would hold the night and that things would be clearer in the light of day. But my friend was in some trouble, and it looked like medical trouble that needed attention sooner rather than later lest the bleeding got out of control. The red was spreading far too fast amid the white. I had to do something, and I had to do it bally quickly."

★

"The shark chose that precise moment to launch another attack, head on, slamming directly into the cage. We rocked and rolled, almost tumbled, but fortunately, and for the time being, we stayed within the bounds of the pentacle etched on the floor. Remembering the success of my chant earlier, I raised my voice again.

"'*Ri linn dioladh na beatha Ri linn bruchdadh na falluis,*'

"'*Ri linn iobar na creadha, Ri linn dortadh na fala.*'

"It had no discernible effect.

"Gault groaned again, and I looked down to see blood drip onto the floor from between his fingers. That only served to enrage the beast in the fog; it came at us again, and again, tossing the cage from side to side and threatening to bowl us over with every strike.

"'Yon beast is after my blood,' Gault said in a momentary lapse in the attack. 'Perhaps you should let me out, old man. There's no sense in both of us getting killed.'

"Even as he said it, the next attack came, the strongest yet, and one that threw the cage clear across the library floor and far out of the protections. The left side of the cage buckled and fell outward, the comforting hum cut off. The link to the generator had been severed.

"We crawled out on our hands and knees before standing up, blind inside a sea of wet gray fog. Blue lightning flashed, and the huge mass of the shark moved, mere feet from where we stood, gliding silently alongside us, its length seeming as if it was never going to end until a tail fin swished in front of my nose and it was gone again.

"Gault stood beside me, clutching an arm that was now bathed almost wholly red. I suddenly had a thought, about his last remark before we had been struck.

"'Maybe it is the blood it is after,' I said. 'Let us give it some, shall we?'

"'Are you mad, man?' Gault said, but I ignored his pleas and grabbed at the hand of his bad arm. His blood pooled, hot in my palm, even as the gray shadow loomed up fast in the fog, coming straight for us.

"The shark's maw gaped open, big enough to swallow both of us whole should the bite be finished.

"I shouted.

"'*Ri linn dioladh na beatha Ri linn bruchdadh na falluis,*
"'*Ri linn iobar na creadha, Ri linn dortadh na fala.*'

"And in the same action I threw blood over the teeth from my hand; one, two, three splashes, as quickly as that. Blue lighting flashed to accompany each splash and a thunderous roar filled the air. The fog seethed and roiled and the great mouth opened even wider. Had I wished to, I could have reached out to touch those razor-sharp teeth as they came within inches of my face.

"I shouted again.

"'*Ri linn dioladh na beatha Ri linn bruchdadh na falluis,*
"'*Ri linn iobar na creadha, Ri linn dortadh na fala.*'

"And this time, almost to my astonishment, but certainly to my most definite relief, the fog began to drift away. The shark's bite did not close on us, and the huge head moved aside, as if it were suddenly confused.

"Once again we saw the length of the Great White slide away in front of us, until it too faded and drifted apart into wisps of misty gray that dispersed quickly as a cold breeze blew in through the library door. The last thing to vanish was three splashes of color, red, where I had daubed the teeth with Gault's blood.

"'Is that it?' Gault said, little more than a whisper. 'Is it truly over this time?'

"I turned toward him to confirm my suspicion that the job was indeed done. I was in time to catch him as his legs gave way and he almost fell.

"I needed to get him to a doctor, and quickly at that. I half-carried him out through the hallway and threw open the front door, intent on hailing somebody, anybody, who might help me with him.

"The captain was too far gone in a faint to see the real

end of the affair, but I was able to relate it to him later as he recovered in the Royal Hospital the next day.

"It is a sight I shall never forget.

"A thin fog, no more than an inch deep, hung over the whole stretch of Cheyne Walk. Ten yards away from my door, and heading fast toward the river, a tall dorsal fin carved through the murk. And right there beside it, to the left, three other fins, small fins, as of young sharks, cavorted and danced alongside until all four were lost to sight in the gloom at the riverbank."

★

Carnacki sat back in his chair and smiled now that the tale was done. He took our questions with good grace over one last round of smokes and drinks, and we were all relieved to discover that the captain was making a fine recovery and hoped to be soon back at sea.

"Now, out you go," Carnacki said, and showed us outside into the cool night air. There was fog away to my left by the river, but I took the long way home via higher ground. Just in case.

The Cheyne Walk Infestation

From the personal journal of Thomas Carnacki, 472 Cheyne Walk, Chelsea.

My good friend Dodgson has done such a heroic job of setting down my experiments, adventures, and misadventures, that I sometimes forget that there are cases he has either found too outlandish, or has been too personally involved in, to do them justice in their writing. As such many of these stories remain, as yet, untold, and that is possibly for the best for the bulk of them.

But in idle moments, I sometimes find a need to have everything I do written and collated, if only for the sake of any that come after me and wish to tread the same paths I have trod. So in that spirit, I will proceed where Dodgson will not, and make a record, when I find the time, of those cases that hold special points of interest to the seeker after knowledge.

★

The case of the infestation from beyond that nearly drove me from my home in Chelsea is one such tale, and to spare Dodgson any qualms about its telling, I shall attempt to set it down here for myself as well as I can remember its particulars. Forgive me if I am not so eloquent in person as my transcriber often attributes to me in prose but I shall try my best to give you the full and proper flavor of the story in my own words.

It begins, as most of these tales do, with a Friday evening dinner party in Cheyne Walk. If I remember correctly, I had a quiet day, mostly spent in study, for supper was a simple one to prepare and did not involve me spending hours in the kitchen. The chaps all arrived promptly, and we set to our fare. The conversation was mostly about rugger, a subject on which I have few opinions, none of them noteworthy.

I was mulling over how best to approach my tale for the evening which was to be a telling of the matter of Grimes Graves, and the thing I found in the darkest deep place there, when I noted that my slices of mutton were tough as old shoe leather. My train of thought was thus more along the lines of admonishing my butcher than on anything metaphysical, and so when Arkwright let out a yelp, I presumed at first that it was a reaction in disgust at the poor fare on his plate. But it did not take me long to discover that the mutton was going to be the least of my worries that evening.

★

I looked up the table to see my friend stab his fork into the body of something that was pale, almost translucent, and was almost as long as my arm, with far too many legs ranked along the length of a sinuous, armored, body. Its internal organs were little more than a pulsating, pink tube that ran through it from front to rear and were clearly visible. It most resembled a monstrously large example of a common millipede, or it would have, had it not been so clearly spectral in nature.

It was not, however, so spectral that it could avoid Arkwright's well aimed fork thrust. He speared it squarely in the back, and it burst with a soft pop, like a soap bubble, before falling, little more now than a rainbow hued flicker in the air, into my table cloth to be lost completely. There was nothing left but a thin oily smear that faded as I leaned forward for a closer look.

As you can imagine, this produced quite the fuss around my table, and we all sat there for long seconds, staring at the spot. Arkwright, unusually for such a renowned trencherman, did not touch his food but leaned across the table, fork poised, waiting to make another thrust should one be required. Everyone held his breath. There was an air of expectancy, as if I had paused at an exciting part of a story, and everyone was waiting on my next word. Unfortunately, I was not in control of this particular tale.

"I say, Carnacki," Arkwright said after a minute or so when there was no recurrence of the phenomenon. "If that was a prank, it was a jolly bad show all round. You could put a chap off his food with that bally nonsense."

I tried to placate my friends, but everyone had seen the thing crawling on the table, and as you can imagine, they had taken a bit of a funk. It is my role in our comradeship to face up to such things after all, and they were more than happy to hear of them over a smoke and a drink, but not to have the bally things turn up in their supper plates.

Arkwright in particular was taking it sorely, and refused to lower the fork. He sat there, old batsman that he is, eyes on the spot where the thing had disappeared, ready and alert to any possible need for action.

The rest of us had all quite lost our appetites, and after ten more minutes passed without any more unwanted apparitions, I managed to mollify them by leading them through to the parlor and plying them with some rather fine brandy I had recently procured.

I had, however, decided to forego the telling of any tales that night, for fear of reminding them of the damnable bug. We conversed quietly about the latest obituaries in *The Thunderer*, and, ever so slowly, everyone became a tad calmer in the familiar, cozy, surroundings around my fire.

The liquor, of course, helped enormously, and I felt that a larger than usual hit to my brandy supplies was a small price to pay for a quiet end to the evening. However, if I thought I was to get away with no further ructions that night, I was quickly to be proved mistaken, and in the worst possible manner.

★

Arkwright had recovered his aplomb sufficiently have moved on from what he considered to be the far too morbid topic of the recently deceased. He was now expounding on one of his favorite subjects, the state of the current England cricket team, a matter on which he was capable of yammering on about for hours if given his head. The rest of us were concentrating on our drinks and smokes, and managing to maintain an air of polite, if not quite rapt, attention, when there was another yelp. This time it came from Dodgson.

The poor chap almost leapt from his chair. I looked down in time to see another of the blasted bug things scuttle away under my drinks cabinet, but I had no time to go after it, for Dodgson had blood pooling in his left shoe at the ankle. The bally thing might be half-spectral, but the other, more solid half had given my friend a dashed serious nip.

Arkwright and the others set to thrashing about under the cabinet with the pokers and fire irons from beside the hearth while I tended to Dodgson as well as I could. The wound wasn't deep, but it was bleeding freely and after I fetched some ointment and bandages from the kit in the dresser and bound him up, there was still a slight seepage of red coming through the white cotton cloth.

Dodgson took it stoically enough, with the help of more of my brandy, although he looked pallid and more than a trifle fearful as he watched Arkwright and the others. They stood around the drink cabinet, freshly poured drinks in one hand, poker or irons in the other, all of them watching the gap between the cabinet and the floor, ready to pounce should anything show itself from beneath.

"Is it dead? Did you get it?" Dodgson said.

"I bloody well hope so," Arkwright bellowed. He turned to me. "What are these blasted things anyway, Carnacki? I know you're not a man for pranks and jests, so tell us straight. Is this serious? Are we in trouble?"

Before I had time to tell him that I was starting to formulate a theory, another dashed thing appeared. This one came up out of the rug in the center of the room, as if it was climbing up through from my wine cellar. And now that I was close enough to hear it, I noticed the high-pitched whine it was giving off, a squeal that grated on my teeth and vibrated in my jaw.

Despite his wound, or perhaps because of it, Dodgson was the first of us to respond to the new arrival in our midst. He stood, stepped forward and, swinging his right foot as if he was back on a rugger field in his youth, punted the bally thing high and hard against the wall of my parlor. The bug hit the angle where the wall met the ceiling with a moist thud, and was already disappearing again, oozing rainbow color in a trail behind it as it slid down the wall. All trace of it was gone before it hit the floorboards.

Dodgson let out a yell of almost childlike joy, but we had no time to celebrate this small triumph. Another of the bug things, its feet solid enough to be scratching and scuttling on the floorboards like a dozen hungry mice, came out fast from the corner nearest the bay window. Arkwright stamped down on that one with a stout boot, but two more were already advancing from the hearth, and there was a third running about under the table that Jessop was trying to get with my pair of long coal tongs.

I was, for my own part, dashed curious as to the nature of these manifestations, and would even have welcomed some time to study their behavior more closely. But with my friends in the room, and Dodgson already a walking wounded, I decided that discretion was most definitely the better part of valor.

"It might be best if we beat a hasty exit, chaps," I said. "Let's get you to a place of safety, then I can return and deal with these intruders in the right and proper manner."

Arkwright set about one of the two from the hearth, clubbing it into mere vapors and oily residue with a poker.

"Whatever you say, old chap," he replied. "Dashed dull sport in any case. They don't even put up much of a fight."

They might not be 'good sport' in Arkwright's parlance, but they were about to make up for that by attacking in some numbers. More arrived, from every direction, up through the floorboards and rugs, out from the wainscoting. Several fell through the ceiling, although those popped and burst as soon as they hit the floor. Within seconds there was a score and more of the damnable things scurrying all around us.

The chaps were now flailing around with the fireside utensils and stomping their feet in a grotesque facsimile of a music-hall dance routine as they tried to stop the scuttling things from closing in enough to give them a nip to equal that which Dodgson had received. More of the bugs poured through the walls. I lost count at forty when I had to lunge aside to avoid one that was intent on dropping on my head from the chandelier above.

We were in serious danger of being completely overrun, and it was only a matter of time before one or more of us would get wounded, or worse.

I let out a rallying cry.

"Into the hall, chaps. Last one out, slam the door behind them."

We beat a hasty retreat. Dodgson was tardier then the others and I was preparing to go back in to check on him when he appeared at the doorway. He had the small scuttle I use for shoveling coal in one hand and a full bottle of my best Scotch in the other.

"I thought both of these might come in handy," he said with a grin, even as he dispatched another of the beasts that was approaching his left foot. He stomped down on it, leaving a shimmering rainbow smear on the floor, then pulled the door shut behind him.

It closed with a slam that rang all through the house, then silence fell.

★

"What now, old man? Jessop said, as we stood there in my hallway in the sudden quiet.

I waited for a few seconds to see if anything was going to come through the wooden panels of the door before answering. My first thought was to open the outside door and shoo all the chaps out into the street in the accustomed manner, to leave me to sort out the problem without having to worry about their safety. But that option was quickly closed to me. More of the dashed things came out of the doorframe and some even rose up from the stone slabs between the front door and our position. We all had to step back sharpish to get out of their way.

Once again I heard the high-pitched whine, and now that it was coming from more than one of the beasts, it sounded less of a formless wail and more like some kind of communication. If I'd had the time right then, I might even to have been able to discern a pattern to it. But time was not something in great supply at that particular moment; the beasts at the doorway skittered and scratched across the floor, all heading towards us, as if impelled by a single purpose. At the same time, I heard another sound, a great scratching and tearing from beyond the closed parlor door, as if a veritable army of the things was ripping at the wood on the other side trying to get through.

"To the library, chaps," I shouted, "and be quick about it. We need to get ourselves into my protections, and I need to find some bally time to think."

I took the lead; Arkwright brought up the rear. My old friend took some degree of pleasure from slashing at the scuttling things with the long poker, wielding it like a cricket bat and sending the bugs either popping like bubbles or flying to all corners with a variety of sweeps and drives.

The other chaps were not tardy in following my lead, and I quickly got us all into my library and had the stout door closed behind us. A survey of the room showed that it appeared to be free of any infestation, for the time being at least.

"Arkwright, are you okay to guard the door for a minute?" I asked.

He nodded.

"Bring them on; I have some more boundaries in me yet." He swung the poker alarmingly to emphasize the point, and I could see by the color in his cheeks that his blood was up.

I bade the others stand inside the protective marquetry circles I have inscribed in the center of the floor in the library. They were reluctant at first, but as soon as the scratching and scuttling started on the outside of the library door they did as was requested with some alacrity.

I made sure they knew the seriousness of our plight, and the necessity of staying inside the inner circle, then I headed for the cupboard under the stairs. I knew I had to move fast as the scratching from out of the hallway was frantic now, accompanied by the high noise that now sounded more than ever like communication, or perhaps song.

Luckily the pentacle was all present and correct in its box, and I had an almost fully charged battery in the cupboard alongside it.

If I'd had a bit more time, I might have ventured downstairs to the cellar to fetch the diesel generator, but that that option was not open to me. I made do with what I had, and set about placing my wires along the lines of the pentacle and my valves in the peaks and troughs. I kept an eye on Arkwright at the door. He stood at alert, poker raised, a batsman waiting for a ball to come down at him, but as yet nothing had ventured through from the hallway.

I had taken my gaze off him, and was almost finished setting up the electric pentacle when I heard the first soft thud and turned to see Arkwright finishing a cover drive that had sent one of the beasts flying against the wall to his right. Then it was all hurry and flight as Arkwright beat a retreat across the floor.

The bugs squeezed, one might almost say oozed, through the door, like ghostly phantoms that only became solid once they reached the library itself. But once inside they started to scuttle and scratch, five, ten, twenty or more so that Arkwright was sore pressed to defend against them. Despite his enthusiasm for the task, my friend was close to being cut off from any possible retreat to the defenses.

★

"Arkwright, get back here; I'm ready." I shouted.

I wasn't quite, but his predicament was such that I was as ready as I was going to be. Arkwright stepped backward, three quick steps without looking where he was going. He almost trod on my blue valve, and I had to reach out and stop him, then make sure he stepped over the lines and into the circle. By this time the dashed bug things were scuttling all around us.

I had time to connect up the battery and throw the switch. The valves hummed into life and the green one flared as one of the creatures threw itself forward, only to be dispersed and torn into rainbow hued dust and shadows as it crashed against my pentacle's defenses.

More of the things crawled and scuttled into the room, coming through the door, out of the walls, up through the floor and even out of the bally books on the shelves. They were all much of the same size, being almost two feet long and slightly sinuous, and within a minute there were scores, possibly hundreds of them, all milling around my library, over the chairs, up and down the book cases. They scratched and scuttled, the sound of their feet keeping time with the rhythm of their song that was loud even above the hum of my valves.

I turned from the scene to look at the other four chaps. They appeared to be steady enough. None of them had taken a funk at the turn of events, but they were all looking to me, expecting either an explanation or a plan of attack.

At that precise moment, I had neither.

★

The things continued to scuttle, but for now they were keeping away from the outer circle of the defenses. I was confident in my equipment's ability to keep us safe, for the time being. But these bug things were now definitely more aggressive, and more solid, and some of them were much less transparent, their outer shells darkening, their inner workings being hidden from view. Whatever I was going to do, I had a feeling that it was best to do it quickly.

I took inventory of what we had brought with us on our forced retreat.

Arkwright still had his poker in hand, Dodgson had the scuttle, and Jessop was wielding the pair of long tongs as if he held a dagger. Taylor had no weapon, and looked rather flushed, but he gave me a thumbs-up to tell me he was dealing with this unprecedented situation. Dodgson also had the Scotch, and between us we had our pipes, several pouches of tobacco and plenty of matches so we were not short of small comforts.

I took the time spent in thinking to fill and light a pipe as I tried to gather my thoughts. It was a bit of a tight squeeze inside the pentacle with us all standing in a circle facing each other, and I knew of old the strain on ankles and legs of standing watch in such vigils.

"Sorry about the lack of chairs, chaps, but we could be here for a while. We should get as comfortable as we can manage."

I sat down, cross-legged, and the others followed suit. Arkwright laid the poker across his lap, and looked like a knight of old, sword at hand, ready for his next battle. Jessop and his coal irons did not quite radiate the same military demeanor, and unlike Arkwright, he was happy to place his makeshift weapon on the floor at his side and ignore it.

Dodgson inspected his wound. The bleeding had stopped but I saw him wince and take a slug from the Scotch bottle when he touched a finger to the bandages. I had seen the damage the bug's nip had done. I knew it was going to be tender and painful for days yet to come. I hoped there was no infection present, and that the wound would not start to bleed any more profusely. In the rush I had forgotten to bring the medical kit, and it was still sitting in the parlor where I had left it in our hasty retreat.

★

Between the library door and the pentacle there was now a teeming throng of the millipedes, all writhing and scratching around and over each other. Ever so often one would approach the pentacle and attempt to breach the circles, but one or other of my valves would flare and hiss, and the thing would dissolve away into the oily rainbow vapors. If they had all attacked at once, the defenses might well have been enough to ensure their total annihilation but they showed no sign of any coordinated effort now, apart, that is, from their singing.

Now that I had time to stop and consider it, I heard that it was indeed structured more like a song than any other kind of communication. There was a certain rhythm and cadence to it that was almost familiar, but I could not quite being to mind where I might have heard it before. I also, on closer inspection of the creatures, discovered where the sound came from. The long millipedes rubbed their rearmost pairs of legs together rapidly to and fro, nearly too fast for the eye to catch. That was what was causing the droning whine that now filled the library and echoed around us.

"What now?" Arkwright asked again. He took the bottle of Scotch from Dodgson, had a slug of his on and passed it around the circle. I waited until we had all partaken before replying.

"As I said, we are safe here for the time being. And I

need some time to think, if you chaps are comfortable in the meantime?"

Dodgson smiled, although there was definitely pain in his eyes.

"We've all heard your stories, Carnacki," he said. "I'm sure you'll find a way to get us out of this mess. It's a pity we didn't think to bring some more of your liquor and some glasses with us."

"At least nobody brought any of that awful mutton," Arkwright said with a grin, and the chaps all had a good laugh at my expense. I let them have it, for seeing them in such good spirits was worth it.

After a minute, we all fell silent, each lost in our own thoughts as we smoked and passed around the Scotch. I puffed on my pipe and watched the beasts writhing all around us. I saw with dismay that where they scuttled and climbed they left behind more of that oily, glistening trail of theirs, one that was already drawing a crazed roadmap of sorts all over the spines of my treasured books. I was already going to be faced with a lengthy job cleaning up after this, and I needed to come up with something fast to avoid it getting any worse.

I could still discern no pattern in their movements, and although the hum and throbbing of their communication continued, the origin of the blasted song continued to elude me. I was now completely sure that I knew it, and it was at the back of my mind, just out of reach.

★

I was on my third pipe, and we were almost out of Scotch, when it came to me. The realization wasn't anything of my own doing, but a jogging of my memory from an external source. In this case, it was the muffled sound of the tolling of the church bell along the street to mark midnight. As soon as the bell sounded, the memory came back to me of where I had heard the same beats and throbs, the same chorus.

I had been in a warehouse in Shoreditch where I had met an ancient spectral worm that was both freed or entrapped depending on the cadence of the chimes of the local church bells. These beasts in my library were singing the same thing, and even as the memory came, I remembered the old song that the beats followed.

"Oranges and Lemons Say the Bells of St. Clements."

I also realized, almost immediately, that I had a possible solution to our current problem.

Arkwright must have seen it in my face.

"Look, chaps, Carnacki has had a brainstorm."

Of course, now that they had taken note, there was nothing for it but to tell them what was on my mind. I reminded them of the particulars of the Shoreditch case, and my theory, very recently formulated, that something, perhaps even a small part of the worm itself, had not been completely vanquished that day. Some part of it had stayed with me, followed me, and was even now making itself at home.

Dodgson in particular had a strong memory of the details of that case, perhaps due to his having transcribed it in such detail in his writings.

"You defeated the worm with your phonographs, did you not? Are you suggesting something similar might work here with these bugs?"

I nodded.

"Yes, indeed. If these bally things are from the same plane as yon worm, then it stands to reason that they will be affected by the same rhythms and notes as the larger beast. But it is not that I intend to do something similar. It is rather that I intend to so something exactly the same. I still have the same wax cylinders I used in Shoreditch when I made the recordings necessary to banish the worm, and I can use them again."

Of course this raised the morale of the chaps considerably, so I was rather disappointed to have to let them down so quickly.

"There is, however, one small problem. I do indeed have the cylinders and the phonographs from the Shoreditch case. But they are in the bottom cabinet of the dresser. And the dresser is in the parlor."

★

Arkwright, stout fellow that he is, immediately got to his feet and swished the poker in the air.

"Tell me what to fetch, and I'll go and get them," he said.

"If it were only that simple, I might consider allowing you the privilege," I replied. "But it must be me to go. There are over twenty cylinders in the cabinet, and only I know which ones will be required."

Dodgson spoke up.

"You cannot step out there among them, man," he said. "I can attest only too well to the fact that they'll give you a nasty nip, and that was just one of them. There might be hundreds of the boogers between you and the dresser in the parlor."

"And yet, I must go," I replied. "I can see no other course of action. And we cannot sit here forever."

This time it was Arkwright who spoke up.

"Then you'll be needing some kind of diversion, old chap," he said, and swished the poker about again, as if eager to be at it.

I could not allow him to leave the circle, I had already decided that much. But he had given me another idea. A diversion was exactly what was needed.

"You lads all know the 'Oranges and Lemons' song, don't you?"

They all nodded their heads.

"Then sing it. Sing as loudly as you can. I do believe it might have an effect."

Part of me was wondering, even as I said it, if I had not hit on a kernel of truth. I had indeed intended it as a diversion, for them though, not for me, something to keep them occupied while I did what had to be done. But as soon as Arkwright started to bellow, and the others joined in, I knew we were on to something.

The creatures stopped scurrying. Long feelers on either side of their heads rose, as if tasting the air, and they appeared to be somewhat confused. The chaps kept singing loudly, and the beasts all came to a stop. I got the impression they were listening.

It was now or never.

I joined the others in song and stepped out of the pentacle.

"Oranges and lemons, Say the bells of St. Clements."

★

The millipede things backed away as I stepped into them, before filling the gap at my back as I passed. They showed no sign of attempting to attack me. I turned and gave the chaps a thumbs-up, still singing as I walked quickly to the library door.

"You owe me five farthings, Say the bells of St. Martin's."

I don't know quite what I was expecting to find on the other side of the door, but it proved to be more of the same. When I stepped into the hallway I was faced with a carpet of sluggish, almost docile, millipedes, all testing the air with their feelers and all seemingly confused by our singing. I put some extra gusto in it as I headed across the hall for the parlor door.

"When will you pay me? Say the bells of Old Bailey."

Whether it was the dampening effect of the walls between us or if it was the distance from the pentacle, I could not say, but the squirming beasts in the parlor were a tad more lively than the ones in the library, and they milled around with greater purpose. I could hear their song louder than I could that of the chaps across the hall in the library.

I kept a close watch on my immediate surroundings as I picked my way through the bugs to the dresser and I sang, bellowing as loudly as Arkwright, louder than I would ever have managed in childhood.

"When I grow rich, Say the bells of Shoreditch."

The swarming things were at least staying well way from my ankles, and fortune favored me as I reached the dresser and looked in the lower cabinet; my phonographs were where I'd remembered them to be, as were the cylinders. I had cause to be grateful for my own efficiency, for they were all labeled with dates, times and identifiers and I was quickly able to lift out the four I was after and stow them in the phonograph boxes.

I debated only taking back one of the boxed machines as they were dashed heavy and awkward to carry, but I had needed both to deal with the Shoreditch worm, so both it had to be.

I kept singing as I turned back toward the parlor door.

"When will that be? Say the bells of Stepney."

Whether they had grown used to our singing, or even bored by the cacophony, the beasts were milling around with more intent now, and one scurried right at my legs before I reached the door. I gave it as hard a kick as my balance would allow and kept moving, kept singing.

"I do not know, Says the great bell of Bow."

I had to stomp and kick my way back through the hallway, and by the time I entered the library again the millipedes were all looking in my direction. I broke into a run. At the same time Arkwright leapt out of the circle, swinging the poker, not with a batsman's finesse, but like a barbarian swordsman intent on hacking his enemies to pieces. His bellow was loud and furious.

"Here comes a candle to light you to bed. And here comes a chopper to chop off your head."

Arkwright held the things at bay long enough for both of us to step back into the circle. Four of the millipedes leapt forward, intent on joining us, but as soon as they hit the air above the pentacle's lines they fizzled and popped, and fell apart into rainbow dust.

The first part of my plan was complete. I had retrieved the phonographs. It was now time to see if putting my theory into practice was going to reward me for my perilous actions.

★

The chaps kept singing while I got the phonographs wound and the cylinders in place, but the millipedes had quickly developed immunity to our vocal charms and were now swarming with frightening speed. I had left the doors open on my return from the parlor, having had both hands full, so that gave the things free run of the whole stretch of parlor, hallway and library. They poured through in a tumbling wave and soon the library was over a foot deep in squirming, wriggling, bugs.

The press of their bodies meant that more and more of them now came into contact with the edge of my defenses and they popped and fizzled and hissed with increasing frequency as yet more of the blighters arrived from through in the parlor.

I saw panic in Dodgson's face as the encroaching millipedes pressed ever closer to us. The valves flared in bright flashes, yellow, green and blue, lighting up the rafters of the ceiling above like fireworks. If I was going to do something, it would have to be now, for I heard the valves start to whine and complain under the strain.

I made sure the first phonograph was wound up fully, and started it off. The peals of the old bells of East London filled the room. I sang along, and the others joined in again.

"Oranges and Lemons say the bells of St. Clements."

The millipedes backed away, slowly retreating from the protections.

★

But their retreat wasn't happening fast enough. Yes, they were retreating; I saw one seem to back away through a shelf of books, leaving more of the oily residue behind. They were still retreating when the first cylinder came to its end. But in the scant few seconds it took me to get the second phonograph to start up, they had already encroached again toward the pentacle, even despite the fact that we were all singing and shouting at the top of our voices.

I started up the second phonograph and the beasts retreated again, only to return when the machine wound down and I started up the other one. I could not get them to retreat far enough, and when I tried playing the two machines with an overlap it did not have the desired effect. The bugs stopped retreating, and did not come forward, but sat, in a watching circle, some eight feet away from the pentacle.

It became like the steps of some bizarre ritualistic dance. Backward and forward they went across the library floor as I played first one, then the other cylinder in rotation.

We had reached a stalemate, one I was unsure how to break, until I had another epiphany.

I had wondered earlier whether the beasts might not self-immolate against the defenses. While I had been worried that the valves and defenses would not survive a slow, steady wave of attack after attack by the beasts, I began to wonder what might happen if they all came in one great rush? Might that not lead to a mass suicide?

Perhaps I might even be able to provoke them into doing so.

I motioned to the chaps that they should keep on singing while I modified the phonographs. It was a simple matter, as they were already equipped to run both forward and backward through the sounds on the cylinders. I set them to run backwards, wound them both up, and set them both going at once.

The result was immediate. As if simultaneously drawn and maddened by the noise, the pale millipedes swarmed and rushed, a wall over four feet high of them, dashing themselves against the pentacle, bursting and popping like water drops on a hot skillet.

The valves flared and blazed and the wails of the attacking millipedes were almost drowned out by the screeching whine from my crystals. Wave after wave of attack came. My green valve popped and faded, going dim without warning, and I did not have any spares on me.

First one, then another of the beasts came through, as if squeezing from out of a dashed tight spot. Arkwright stepped over to that side and quickly disposed of them with his poker, then had to move quickly to stop another scuttling through between his legs.

And still the attack came, and the lights blazed and the valves whined and Arkwright stomped and slashed and cursed, loud enough to be heard by us all. The valves whining went up a notch and I knew I was straining the defenses to limits they had never before been tested under. I was starting to fear the worst when another wave of attack was launched. I winced involuntarily as a three feet high wall of squirming, thrashing, millipedes hit the outer protection.

The defensive valves all blew out at once, but in doing so, they all gave out a last burst of light. There was a yellow glare as bright as the sun, and when my eyes adjusted we were alone in the pentacle amid a sea of rainbow vapors and mist that were even now sinking to the floorboards to leave only an oily residue as evidence the millipedes had ever existed.

My plan had worked.

★

It was quite some time before the chaps were calm enough to understand that it was over.

"That was a jolly close call, Carnacki," Arkwright said.

I patted him on the shoulder.

"It would have been a damned sight closer without your help, old man," I replied. "But I think we are safe now. Here, I shall prove it."

I stepped out of the protections. Nothing happened. There was no recurrence of the bugs, no sign of any hum or throb. The only thing left of them was the faintest gleam of oily residue like slug trails across the floor and up the bookcases, but I was glad to see that even that was now fading away into nothingness

I went and fetched more liquor, and five glasses this time, from the parlor, but could not get the chaps to leave the pentacle until they had all smoked a pipe and we had polished off the best part of another bottle of Scotch.

There was still no recurrence of the millipedes, no scuttling from the other rooms. I saw Dodgson eye the doorway with some trepidation as I suggested the coast was clear.

"Are you sure they are all gone?" he said.

I nodded.

"As sure as I can be, and after we get you all home I shall enhance the protections to encompass the whole house, for a while at least, just to be careful."

We finished off the bottle of Scotch between us before I could convince them to step out of the defenses, and when they did so and were not attacked by any more bugs, they were all rather keen to be on their way immediately afterward.

When I finally ushered them out the door I saw by the big clock in the hall that it was almost three in the morning; a much later conclusion to our dinner party than was normal.

Arkwright was the last to leave.

"Are all your adventures this much fun, old chap?" he said. "Because if you need any more beasties hit with a poker,

I'm your man for the job."

We laughed then, for the first time in several hours, and I sent him off into the night with a smile.

"Out you go," I said.

An Unexpected Delivery

It had been one of those hot, almost sultry, days of haze and lingering stench that sometimes affects the river and the adjoining streets in high summer. Even the short walk down to 472 Cheyne Walk had me hot and bothered and disgusted by the smell assaulting my nose and throat. The stench was so foul that it made me rush ahead faster than I might have done otherwise. I am ashamed to admit it, but I was somewhat in a sweat when Carnacki opened the door and ushered me inside.

A glass of lightly chilled beer helped, as did the relatively cool air inside the house. I do not know how he manages it, but Carnacki's dining room always remains temperate whatever the weather outside, and by the time we gathered for supper at the table I was starting to feel more like myself.

The fare that night was an unusual combination for most of us, starting with a salad of some small, unidentifiable grain containing several vegetables with which I was completely unfamiliar. The main course was darkish meat that tasted rather like mutton but I suspected was goat, braised in sweet, but not sickly liquor, highly spiced, and served on a bed of wheat, dates and figs.

Arkwright, I could tell, was not too impressed with these foreign offerings, but he was far too polite to make any fuss of it at the table. As for myself, I polished it off, finding the heady spices quite to my liking. There was a most delicious partially frozen yogurt and fruit dessert to follow, and I ate Arkwright's portion after finishing off my own, so that by the time we went through to the parlor for drinks and a smoke I was quite full.

The parlor was equally as cool as the room we had left, and there would be no need for a fire that night. I suspected that if the room did cool any farther, all we would have to do to rectify it would be to open a window and let some of the warmer air in from the outside. Our host had a new bottle of scotch to hand, a peaty island malt that none of us had previously sampled, and it went down very nicely as we got our smokes lit and readied ourselves for a tale.

Carnacki did not disappoint us; he started in

immediately.

★

"Our supper tonight was by way of an introduction to the nature of my latest adventure," he began, "for it has a distinctive Egyptian flavor, rather like the goat we have just eaten."

Arkwright looked like he wanted to interject, but that time was passed; it was a house rule that once a story was started, interruptions were most definitely frowned upon. Carnacki continued without a pause.

"It starts early on a Saturday morning with a knock on my front door. This was a month ago now, but you will remember that my tale of the night before had been a long one, and we had all partaken of a tad more scotch than was usual, so I was more fragile than I might have been in other circumstances. I was only recently risen from my bed and not yet ready to face breakfast. Finding an inspector and constable from Scotland Yard on my doorstep did little to make the morning any more palatable.

"The inspector introduced himself as Whittaker of the Yard. He did not offer a name for the man with him, and he asked if he could have a word with me. I could tell by his demeanor that it was something bally serious, so I invited them in and showed them into the library, where I'd been intending to work an a section of the Sigsand until my hangover abated.

"The inspector wasted no time in reaching the point.

"'I believe you know an elderly gentleman by the name of Edwards,' he said. 'A professor of antiquities?'

"'I do indeed,' I replied as I filled a pipe. 'George is an old friend. I have known him for many years and he often has insights into my studies that I do not immediately see for myself.'

"'And these studies of yours,' the inspector said. 'May I ask as to their nature?'

"He was being cagey and still, like a hawk watching for prey. I realized I would have to be careful with my words with this man, for he looked like the type not to miss a trick.

"'My studies are of a historical, spiritual and esoteric

nature,' I replied, waving at the shelves around us in the library. 'As you can see from my collection.'

"He showed no sign of being interested in the books; his eyes never left mine.

"'Morbidly interested in death, are we, Mr. Carnacki?'

"I knew immediately there was no answer to that question I could give that would satisfy him. Instead I tried to get him to come to the point of his visit.

"'There has not been any trouble, I hope?'

"I saw from the inspector's look that there had indeed been trouble, and from the manner in which he continued to study me, I knew that he suspected that I might be somehow involved. His next question merely confirmed my suspicions.

"'Could you tell me where you were between the hours of eight and midnight last night, sir?' he asked.

"I saw from the look he gave me that the trouble was indeed of a most serious nature. I was jolly glad to have an alibi immediately to hand. If I had not, I do believe I might have been hauled down to a damp cell in Scotland Yard right there and then.

"'I was here at home, entertaining some old friends,' I replied.

"He was somewhat surprised to hear it. I do not think he expected me to be able to explain myself quite so easily, and I took him aback for a second before he asked another question.

"'And these friends of yours will confirm that you were present here the whole evening?'

"'They will indeed, to a man. We have regular Friday meets. Last night was no different to many others.'

"'You're sure they will back you up in this matter? I will need their names, in any case.'

"'Certainly,' I replied, and gave the inspector's constable your names and addresses. I think I quite impressed the man by mentioning such pillars of the community as you fellows. And as none of you have brought it up before tonight, I can take it the inspector never followed up on the matter.

"I think by then he was starting to admit that I was not a suspect, and he loosened up a tad when I offered him a smoke. I eventually got the full story, or at least as much of it as he knew, out of him over a pot of tea."

★

"'I'm afraid I have some bad news for you, Mr. Carnacki,' he said, and I had guessed his next words before they were spoken. 'There is never an easy way to break this. Your friend Professor Edwards is dead. The old chap was found at his desk this morning.'

"'I gather, given that you are here so soon afterward to question me, that his demise was not brought on by natural causes?'

"Whittaker sighed.

"'That would have made things so much simpler. No, his passing was not a peaceful one, I'm afraid. The old man appears to have been strangled, and rather viciously at that. The only clue left behind at the scene was a hastily scribbled name in his journal that was obviously his last act. There was only the one word, but it was written clear enough there was no mistaking the name, your name…Carnacki.'

"Of course, hearing that gave me quite a turn, and I could see now why the man had found his way to my door. And I was quite distraught at hearing my old friend had met his end in such violent and distressing circumstances.

"'I shall help you out in any way that I can,' I promised the inspector.

"But I had no information to hand that could help the Yard with their investigation. I had not seen the professor for some weeks, and the last time we spoke, he was deep in the investigation of some new artifact that had come into his possession.

"'This artifact,' the inspector asked when I mentioned it. 'It was valuable?'

"I could almost see his thought processes; such an item might be another clue, possibly even a motive that could be investigated further. I had to disappoint him again.

"'I have no idea of its value, nor even what it might look like. He told me that it was old, and middle-eastern I think, or possibly Egyptian, but beyond that the old chap was playing his cards close to his chest and didn't give me any particulars.'

"'And you still cannot think why he might have chosen to write your name as his last act?'

"I had been racking my brains on that same score since the inspector mentioned it, but I could think of nothing that might help him.

"'The professor shared some of my enthusiasms for the arcane,' I replied. 'I can only think that it might be something along those lines, but as for the particulars, I am sorry to say that I am at a complete loss.'

"The inspector looked weary, and sighed again.

"'Thank you for your time, in any case,' he said.

The constable put his notebook away and both officers rose from their chairs.

At least I was not to be taken away for further questioning. The inspector was satisfied with my answers to his questions, and left me with a request to get in touch should I remember anything that might prove pertinent to their investigation.

"After seeing them out, I went back inside and finally managed to eat some breakfast, my hangover having quite vanished during my questioning. After that I sat in the library with a smoke, wool-gathering and mourning an old friend I would never see again. I was rather startled when there was another knock on the main door not half an hour later.

"I thought it might be the inspector, returned having remembered something he had neglected to ask of me, but instead it was a young lad, no more than ten years old. He looked flushed, red in the face as if he had arrived in quite some rush. He carried a shoebox wrapped in brown paper that he held out toward me as if by way of explanation for his presence.

"'Begging your pardon, sir. I was told to deliver this to you last night but I got a bit behind with another job. I am right sorry for being so tardy. The elderly gent said there would be a shilling in it for me, but given my lateness, there is no payment required.'

"I gave him a shilling anyway for his honesty, and sent him on his way before even looking at the package. I knew right away that I should not have sent the lad off so hastily; the Yard might need to have a word with him.

"The well-wrapped package was addressed to me, and I

immediately recognized the handwriting as belonging to my old friend, Edwards. If the boy who delivered it was to believed, it had been sent from the professor, the previous evening, at some point not long before he saw fit to write my name again, one last time."

★

"I know that you chaps will all say that I should, by all rights, have got in touch with the Yard there and then, for what I had in my hands was most surely evidence in a case involving violence and murder. But I was curious, mightily so, as to why my name had been the last thought in my old friend's mind, and I believed the contents of the package might shed some light on the matter. I decided that I needed to investigate for myself before bothering the inspector with what might, after all, turn out to be something completely unrelated to the professor's death.

"I could not tell by the weight of the box what might lie inside, and shaking it ran the risk of damaging the contents, so I took it through to the dining room and opened it. I did so carefully, so as not to destroy any of the packaging, lest I incur the wrath of the inspector later.

"Edwards had been at his most meticulous in his wrapping. The package was neatly double layered in crisp, newly purchased brown paper and it had been tied with expensive white twine. Inside there was indeed, as I suspected, a shoebox, for a pair of Oxfords from James and Sons of Bond Street, but there were no shoes inside it. There was, however, an envelope addressed to me, and, wrapped tightly inside several layers of tissue paper, I found a palm-sized locket of some antiquity.

"It was mounted on a heavy, gold chain that looked of similar age to the locket itself. The rear side of the thing was burnished silver and flat and the front was a carving done in deepest black jet, depicting a scarab beetle in intricate detail. The locket was obviously meant to open, for there was a finely wrought hinge on the left-hand side. It felt heavy in the hand, courtesy of the jet, and I could imagine that wearing the bally thing around one's neck for any great length of time would prove to be dashed uncomfortable.

"It appeared I had been made recipient of the same artifact I had so recently been discussing with the inspector, and once again I considered whether I should not be handing it over immediately to the Yard as evidence.

"But as I have said, I was mightily curious, and decided that further investigation on my part was still required. On another night I might have broached the hinge there and then. I do not rightly know what stopped me; my old friend's fine hand on the envelope perhaps, or an innate sense of survival. Whatever the case, I opened the envelope first before proceeding any further.

"That single act might have saved my life."

★

Carnacki paused in his story at this point and drew a folded sheet of thick cream-colored paper from his inside jacket pocket.

"I thought it might help, and provide an air of verisimilitude to my tale, if I let you see the letter itself," he said as he opened out the folded paper and read from it.

"My dear Carnacki,

"I must apologize for burdening you with my self-inflicted troubles, but I am afraid that I have been a stupid old fool. I send you this item in the hope it is not too late, and that you might, with your expertise in such matters, be able to avert the fate that even now is reaching for me.

"I shall package it up immediately and send it straight to you. Mayhap it might even save my poor old soul, although I fear matters are already too far along for that.

"I told you I was working on an artifact. What I did not tell you, could not, is that I acquired it by nefarious means.

"The thing you have no doubt by now held in your hand turns up over and over again in the old writings, and I have, over the course of several decades, become a tad obsessed with it. So when I heard a rumor that it had surfaced in our time, I knew it was important, and that I had to have it. I found a man who knew a man who would procure it for me with no questions asked. In doing so I have violated most of the tenets of archaeological research I hold dear, but when you've seen it for yourself, you will understand. I simply had to have it.

"It cost me all that I had, and all that I will ever have. And now that I have seen it, and opened it, the obsession has been lifted from me as if it never existed, and I wish to blazes I had not had it stolen from its owner and brought to me.

"But it is too late now for forgiveness. It is far too late. If you must open it, and knowing you, I think you must, please ensure you are fully protected. It is old, it is dark, and it is angry. And I fear it is coming for me now.

"Forgive me, old friend. I must put this thing in your trust. Do with it what you will.

"But please, for the sake of our friendship if nothing else, be bloody careful.

"Your friend forever,

"Edwards."

★

Carnacki carefully folded the paper up and put it away in his pocket again before continuing.

"Of course, after reading that, there was only one course of action to purse; I knew that I would have to open the bally thing to see what had got the old chap in such fear for his life. But Edward's letter had given me pause for thought, and, again, there was also the fact that I might be destroying, or contaminating, evidence pertaining to his murder.

"This time, I decided that discretion was the better part of valor, and that I should make good on my promise to the inspector to keep him informed. I made a quick visit to the post office and sent a telegram to the Yard, requesting that Whittaker pay me a visit at his earliest convenience, and left the Scarab and the box it came in on the table in the dining room.

"I came through here to the parlor for a snifter and a smoke while I waited. For a while I was even able to settle, lost in reminisces of my poor dead friend, and wondering at the nature of the obsession he had mentioned in his letter. It was an obsession he had hidden so well over the years that he had never once mentioned it to me despite the long hours we had spent in each other's company.

"But the bally locket preyed on my mind, and after a while I could not think of anything but what might await to be found inside the dashed thing, and what it might have to do with Edwards' death.

"And there was still no sign of the inspector returning my message. I felt rather twitchy, and it was a tad too early to take to the bottle for comfort. In the end, I gave in to my impulses, took the scarab locket through to the library, and set the electric pentacle up over the defensive circles I have etched into the hardwood floor.

"I hooked up the strongest of my batteries and switched on, before taking a chair, the scarab, and a magnifying glass, into the heart of the pentacle. I deduced that, just as the pentacle protected me from exterior action, so too it would serve to protect me from anything the scarab had to surprise me with."

★

"As I was stepping inside the circles, the blue valve flared very slightly and dimmed again, but I thought nothing of it at the time. My whole attention was now on the scarab, and how I might open it without doing any damage to the locket.

"I sat down, and, ever so carefully, pried it open with my thumbnail. The old hinge creaked rather alarmingly, but the locket came open without a hint that it might break. The inside of both halves was burnished silver that had been polished to an almost mirror-like sheen, and the back piece was engraved in tiny, delicately inscribed, verse. I was able to make out the words, but only with the aid of my magnifying glass.

"I had expected hieroglyphs, but what I got was Greek. I translated along in my head as I read, somewhat slowly, as it had been quite some length of time since my last reading of that ancient language.

"'*All people who enter this tomb, make evil against this tomb and destroy it, may the crocodile be against them in water and snakes against them on land. May the hippopotamus be against them on water and the scorpion against them on land.*'

"It was a curse, of course, and a dashed ancient one at that. Now that I had read that far, and had a good look at the artifact itself, I suspected that the scarab locket had once hung around the neck of a member of Egyptian royalty, and had probably been purloined from there when the tomb was opened. I could now also understand, at least in part, what had so obsessed my old friend, for it was indeed a thing of great beauty, even discounting its obvious historical importance.

"What I did not yet understand was how Edwards had allowed the curse to put him in such an obvious funk, or how it might have somehow contributed to his demise. I have come across many such warnings in my studies, but I could see nothing that might frighten an experienced old hand like Edwards, or lead to his gruesome death.

"I was thinking that this whole bally experience might be as a result of the old prof's overwrought imagination when the blue valve flared alarmingly, so bright that it blinded me momentarily. At the same instant I felt tightness at my throat. Firstly, it was little more than a difficulty in drawing breath, but that quickly turned into a full-on assault, gripping at me as if I wore a noose. All too quickly the constriction became so severe that the pain was excruciating and blackness crowded in, the darkness of death swelling up, ready to take me down and away into the black."

★

"It was pure instinct that saved me. I stood quickly, dropping the scarab onto the seat of the chair. I felt, frantic now, around my neck. There was nothing there for me to take hold of. But it continued to tighten, and if I did not do something about it immediately, I would never take another breath.

"With the last of the air left to me already wheezing out of my chest and blackness creeping at the edges of my vision, I stepped over the circles and out beyond the defenses onto the library floor.

"The constrictive force at my neck and throat was lifted as if it had never been there and I was able to draw in a huge gulp of air. I stood, hands on knees, for a minute or so, drawing in whooping breaths until I felt able to stand upright again.

"It was only then that I noticed that the blue valve was

pulsing, a definite rhythm, like a slow heartbeat. The air inside the pentacle above the still open scarab and the chair swirled and thickened, as if a dense fog was rising from within the locket itself. The blue valve kept pulsing and, fed by the light, the fog coalesced and took form.

"A serpentine body slithered, its flanks pulsing in time with the blue valve as it solidified into something that was most definitely tangible. Within a minute a large, thick-bodied snake was coiled around the legs of the chair. In circumference the thickest part of the body was larger than one of my thighs and I guessed it would be near twenty feet, if not more, in length should it be able to straighten itself. It raised a head the size of two fists put together and looked straight at me. The hood of the huge cobra, for that was indeed what it was, opened as it hissed, slithering out a moist forked tongue and showing me its fangs. The sound grated on my ears like fingernails on a chalkboard.

"I remembered the words I read in the locket.

"'*All people who enter this tomb, make evil against this tomb and destroy it, may the crocodile be against them in water and snakes against them on land*'

"I had narrowly escaped being beset by one of the very beasts mentioned in the warning.

"I realized something else as I watched the serpent breathe in and out in time with the pulsing of my valve. I was looking at the thing that had got poor Edwards.

"Once my breathing had returned to something approaching normal, I took a step back toward the defenses, trying to get a closer look at the thing. I was immediately thankful that I had the foresight to examine the amulet inside my defenses; the green and yellow valves flared wildly as the serpent tried to strike at me, and blue sparks of static electricity flew around the serpent's form like bottled lightning. I had inadvertently caged the beast inside the circles.

"But as I stood there watching it writhe and thrash in its attempts to escape, I didn't have a bally clue as to what I should do next."

★

Carnacki stopped again, and rose from his chair. We, from long familiarity with the beats and rhythms of his tales, knew this was our cue and we all followed his lead, moving to refill our glasses.

Arkwright, as ever, was keen to fill the lull in the story with questions. Carnacki was also, as ever, expert at avoiding giving away any clue as to the direction the story might take toward its conclusion. As a matter of fact, this kind of gentle sparring between the two of them often did much to increase our anticipation for the remainder of the tale to come, and tonight was no exception.

As eager as children at bedtime, we settled with our glasses charged and our smokes lit, ready for the rest of the story.

★

"I was not given any time to consider my next action, for that decision was taken from me by a loud knock on the street door. I had one last look at the defenses, trying to convince myself that they would hold in my absence, and closed up the library before heading to answer. I had no way of gauging the strength of the serpent, and all that I really knew was that I had a few hours left in the battery that powered the valves. I could only hope it would give me long enough to come up with a solution.

"Inspector Whittaker was waiting on the doorstep when I opened the door, and it was only then that I recalled I had sent for him; my encounter with the serpent had taken up all of my concentration.

"'You have new information for me? Have you remembered something?' he asked.

"'Let us say, there has been a development.' I replied.

I invited him in, showed him into the parlor, and over a smoke, explained about the package I had received and the manner in which it had come to me. Of course, he asked about the contents so I fetched the letter and the box from the dining room. His left eyebrow raised quizzically as he read it and then read it again, more slowly the second time.

"'And what was inside the box?' he asked after he was

done.

"'That is rather difficult to describe,' I replied. 'It was an Egyptian Scarab locket, of some great antiquity.'

"He handed the note back to me.

"'I too have some information to impart,' he said. 'I believe we have uncovered the locket's rightful owner. A businessman in Cairo has been in touch with the Yard to file a complaint against your Professor friend. We have had the chap's credentials checked and he seems to be exactly who he claims to be, a man of some wealth and influence in Egypt. He has made an allegation of theft of an unusual item of jewelry, and from the description he has given to us, I believe we must be talking about this self-same pendant that is now in your possession. I assume you still have it?'

"'I do indeed,' I replied, as yet unsure how I was going to explain what was coming next.

"'Where is it now?' he asked.

"'It is in my library.'

"'And may I see it?'

"That was the question I had not wanted to hear. I stalled for time, my mind racing.

"'Do you have any clue as to the nature of my particular area of expertise, inspector?'

"'I know you are regarded as an expert in things esoteric and strange, and that you have the ear of some people in high places that place credence in your ability.' He smiled. 'One hears stories, even in my own small area of expertise. Besides, I try not to call on a chap without knowing at least something about him.'

"I decided to go with my instincts again, which told me that the inspector would at least consider what I had to say and not dismiss me out of hand.

"'What I have in the library certainly comes under the term esoteric,' I said. 'I must ask you to prepare yourself, and I need your promise that you will not do anything hasty. It could be dangerous, for both of us.'

"'Is anyone in trouble?'

"'Only ourselves, and only if we are not careful,' I replied.

"'Then you have my promise,' the inspector replied. 'I

am not a hasty man.'"

★

"He kept his word when I showed him into the library, although I think it was more wonderment, awe, and a hint of fear that struck him immobile rather than any predisposition to not be hasty.

"'What in blazes is it?' the inspector whispered after a time.

"My pentacle sent washes of color all around the room, across the wooden floor, over the ranks of high books and shelving, and swirled, like rainbow clouds, across the ceiling. The serpent was still inside my circles, still contained, lying coiled around the legs of the chair in the center. The blue valve pulsed, beating in time with the sinuous breathing of the beast that looked at me with unblinking eyes. It had stopped attacking the defenses but somehow this cold, uncaring stare was worse, for it told me that the serpent was ready to wait me out, and I was only too aware of the finite life of my battery.

"The inspector was still waiting for an answer to his question.

"'I was trying to ascertain the nature of the thing before you came to the door,' I said, and laid out the situation for him. 'It appears my defenses are holding it, but the battery will not last forever. And as to your question, I believe it is what a layman or a newspaperman would call the external physical realization of a curse. To put it in my terms, it is something from the Outer Dark realms beyond our own that has attached itself to the locket and brings harm to those that would dare to open it without having an understanding as to its nature.'

"'I see. Or rather, I don't. But I trust my eyes, and I'll take your word on the curse part. The main question is, how do we get rid of it?'

"'In theory, it can be dispatched back to its sleep by returning it to its rightful owner so that he in turn can return it to the place where it originally slept, dormant and controlled.'

"'We can probably do that given we now know about our businessman in Cairo.'

"'Yes indeed. That is where it must be sent. But first, we

must get the locket closed again. And that means going inside the pentacle and evading the serpent.'"

★

"We stood there in the library smoking while I contemplated the problem. I was also watching for any sign of dimming in the valves, for by my calculation, it was close to being run down. The inspector picked up on my concern, but from a slightly different perspective.

"'What happens if you let the battery run down on your contraption?' he asked.

"'I have been wondering that myself,' I said. 'I believe that when the protections are gone, the serpent will be free to fulfil the curse, and it will be coming after me, as I was the last one to open the bally thing.'

"'Probably not a good idea to wait until the last minute then,' he said, and I rather agreed with him on that score.

"The serpent was keeping its gaze directed on me, and I felt the baleful stare, almost as a physical force pressing on me. I stepped closer to the pentacle. The head came up, the large oval cowl opened out and a forked tongue tasted at the defenses, causing the yellow and green valves to flare wildly before settling again.

"'I think he likes you,' Whittaker said sardonically.

"I must admit he was taking the situation jolly well for a policeman. He did not seem in any fear now. He was more curious as to the nature of the thing I had trapped there in the library. He joined me in considering the best way to go about ridding ourselves of it, as if it was another puzzle that could be solved with the right approach and a number of clues to chew on. We talked through several scenarios, and I was pleased to discover an open mind, and an analytical one at that. Indeed, he was the first of us to suggest an approach of action.

"'I've been watching his eyes, Carnacki,' Whittaker said. 'He's following you everywhere.'

"'I've noted that too. But I'm not sure how that changes anything.'

"Whittaker smiled, but didn't let me in on his thinking.

"'Stay right where you are, old bean. I want to check

something.'

"He sidled away from my side, circling the room until he was on the opposite side of the pentacle from me; I could barely see him through the washes of color from the valves. The serpent never shifted its gaze from me.

"'Here we go, then. Get ready,' the inspector shouted.

"'Ready for what?' I called back, but he was already on the move.

"He strode forward, stepped over the defensive circles, and reached for the locket where it sat on the chair."

★

"The serpent's response was immediate; it struck out at him, but in one move the inspector had his left arm up to defend his face while his right grabbed the locket, snapped it shut one handed and threw it, chain and all, out of the defensive circles.

"The blue valve blazed, almost blinding as the amulet passed through the boundary of the circles, but the man's throw had been so straight that all I had to do was raise my hand to catch it, and in a second the locket was nestling there in my palm.

"Whittaker's ploy had, however, not proved totally successful, for although the locket was closed, the beast was still imprisoned inside the pentacle. Even now the serpent was upon him, great coils, already tightening, thrown around his legs, hips and chest and heading inexorably for his throat. The blue valve pulsed and blazed, and the serpent's eyes grew brighter in turn. I did not consider that to be a coincidence.

"I stepped forward, locket still in hand, and stamped down, hard, on the blue crystal, which cracked, splintered, and fell apart in a shower of blue dust. The rest of the valves all blazed as one, and shrieked, like a gull denied bread. A great black coldness washed like a wave through the room.

"I felt a momentary tightening at my throat, but it was weak, and passed quickly. When I looked down there was just the pentacle, the valves all dull and still now, and Whittaker, lying, gasping for breath, beside the chair in the center of the circles.

"He smiled wanly.

"'That went quite well, don't you agree, old man?'

"'I thought you said you weren't a hasty man?' I said as I bent to his aid.

"He croaked rather than spoke in reply as he rose slowly to his feet.

"'And I thought you said there wasn't going to be any trouble.'

★

"Scotch, as it usually does, did the trick of reviving him, although I believe the poor inspector may still be bruised about the body even now, almost a month later. We stayed close to the defenses while we had a drink and a smoke, but there was no sign of any return of the serpent. Once he felt sufficiently recovered, Inspector Whittaker took his leave, taking the locket with him to expedite its return to the rightful owner.

"I have continued to stay close to the defenses myself all through the month, ready to defend myself at the slightest hint of an attack. I already knew, from poor Edwards' experience, that the physical presence of the locket was not required for the serpent to do its worst. But this morning I got a message from the inspector that I could rest easy. I am pleased to say that the locket is back in Cairo and has been returned to the tomb from where it was taken."

★

Carnacki rose, his tale done. As he did so, I saw the patch of skin below the nape of his neck and above the collar. It was still purple and yellow with old, fading bruising, but if it pained my friend, he did not reveal it as he showed us to the door.

"Now, out you go," he said.

A Sticky Wicket

From the personal journal of Thomas Carnacki, 472 Cheyne Walk, Chelsea

I have a tale to relate here in my journal that once again cannot be told to Dodgson and the others after dinner. The reason this time is not one of national security or of saving the reputation of a Duke or Duchess. Rather, it is a much more prosaic matter. By retaining this note only in this written form, and by dint of having it locked safely away here in my personal journal, it will keep a secret that is only known to myself and one other of our dining group. It is for the best that it remains that way.

It is also for the best if I start at the very beginning.

★

It was a month ago after a story, and Arkwright held back from departing to have a word with me after the others had gone.

"I need a favor, old chap," he said to me, somewhat sheepishly. "I've been over and over this in my mind for bally weeks now, and I cannot for the life of me come to any other conclusion but that this matter lies fair and square in your domain. And if you do not help me, it'll be a blasted disaster all round."

Whatever it was that he had on his mind, he appeared to be genuinely upset about it, and of course I could do nothing else but hear him out. We went back to the parlor, I poked the fire to get a bit more life out of it, and over a brandy and cheroot I finally got out of him what the trouble was.

★

"It's the blasted wicket at Carlside, my cricket club," he said. "You know I play there every Sunday? Well, for six home games in a row, since the start of the season, we've lost every bally game. And we've lost them badly at that, by big, almost embarrassing scores. It's not that we're batting like beginners, Carnacki, it's that the ball is doing dashed peculiar things on our home turf. When we bowl, it slows off the pitch and the opposition whack us around the ground, yet when we bat, it's fizzing and popping all around the houses, bouncing up into our faces or straightening up at the ankles to slap us in the pads. We haven't scored more than fifty among the lot of us all summer, we're stuck at the bottom of the Sunday league, and it is all starting to get jolly annoying."

I had not been expecting anything so prosaic, and I was more than a tad relieved to find that my old friend's problem was only one of a game of cricket or two. I tried my damnedest to keep a straight face, but I'm afraid that was one battle I was destined to lose, and my amusement must have showed.

"Dash it, Carnacki, this is no laughing matter," Arkwright said, immediately taking umbrage. He was almost shouting, and had gone quite red in the face. "This is cricket I'm talking about here. It's bally important."

I refrained from suggesting that perhaps more practice on the playing fields and less time in the bar might ensure a better performance, as that wasn't the sort of thing he wanted to hear. Instead, I decided to take him at his word and assume he was right that there was indeed something affecting the outcome of his team's games. I owed my old friend at least that much respect. And as an exercise in detection, I thought that it might even prove interesting.

I poured him another brandy and we lit up another smoke. It was late now, but Arkwright was still muttering away under his breath and I could not let him leave in a state. I quizzed him for another quarter of an hour, but learned little else of substance beyond the fact that it was all dashed peculiar, and that the poor chap was indeed in quite a worry over the matter.

"I can't sleep for the thought of it, old man," he said.

"We won the league last year. It would a damnable, intolerable, disaster to come bottom the very next season."

I promised to go down to Carlside with him that very Sunday to see what could be seen, and that settled Arkwright somewhat, although he was still far from his usual voluble self when I finally showed him out as the clock in the hall struck midnight.

★

The following Sunday was a gorgeous, clear, summer day with little wind and the promise of a warm afternoon. Carlside C.C. belongs to the quaint and charming school of local cricket grounds. It was originally built on an expanse of flat common land on the edge of the village some ninety years or so ago. It has an old coaching inn doubling as the clubhouse, a sturdy Norman church with adjoining cemetery over the southern boundary and a slow, meandering, trout stream along the north side in which I imagine many balls have been lost over the years.

I caught the early train down to Kent to arrive in time to be allowed an inspection of the wicket before the match started. Arkwright joined me at the crease, pointing to where this or that ball had misbehaved and caused him or one of his team to lose their wicket. I looked closely, searching for a clue, but I could see nothing untoward on the surface. It looked flat and hard, with no cracks despite the dryness of the soil and thinness of the grass. I anticipated a closely fought match that afternoon.

What I got was anything but close. I sat, sipping some very fine ale and watching Arkwright's team field while their opponents, a burly bunch of farm lads from a neighboring village, dispatched fours and sixes all over the ground. Several balls were lofted for sixes into the trout stream as they piled up over two hundred runs, for the loss of only two wickets in their allotted number of balls. By the end of the innings, the home side were all red in the face with exertion and more than a tad dejected, even before it came to their turn to bat.

As the teams walked in to the clubhouse, a chap with a heavy grass roller went out to prepare the wicket for the second innings. A light tea of sandwiches and ale was taken, and Arkwright looked as glum as I had ever seen him as he prepared for batting.

"Did you see that?" he said as he sat beside me fastening on heavy pads to protect his shins and knees. "We bowled the right line, there was scarcely a bad ball in the lot, and despite that, each of the balls sat up ready to be whacked. I'm telling you, Carnacki, there's some kind of malarkey at work here."

I myself am not an aficionado of the game, but it had looked to me that the other side was made up of good batsmen and that Arkwright was perhaps not quite the good sport he wanted to be. I could not find it in myself to tell him though, so I held my peace at the time. Besides, any response would have been futile, as Arkwright was already walking away from me, heading onto the field of battle to open the batting with his partner.

★

It went well to begin with, for Arkwright at least. Whether it was my presence, or his belligerence at the thought that foul play might have been brought to his beloved game, he set about the bowling attack with quite some gusto. Although his batting partners came and went for low scores, Arkwright stood firm and managed to send some big hits over the boundary rope, one of which came perilously close to clattering against the old Norman church's stained glass windows. For a time it appeared that Arkwright might even win the match on his own. Then there came the thing that made me finally sit up and take notice.

The bowler sent down a slower, spinning ball. Arkwright stepped forward to defend it staunchly, but the ball hit the turf and went backwards for a split second, as if deliberately avoiding the bat, before scuttling forward again, through Arkwright's legs and knocking over middle stump.

★

I saw, even at a distance, that my old friend was almost apoplectic, but he was too good a sport to argue with the umpire, and he strode off to warm applause on a score of seventy-five. Unfortunately, the rest of his team could not manage that much among the rest of them, and Carlside went down by over sixty runs not too long afterward.

Drinks were taken, congratulations were given, and Arkwright maintained the dignity of a sporting loser long enough to see the winning side fed and watered and sent home. It was only as darkness settled on the ground that he allowed his feelings to be shown. Even then, he waited until I was the only other person left with him in the quiet bar.

"Did you see that bally ball?" he said.

"I did. Dashed bad luck, old man," I replied.

"Luck? Luck had nothing to do with it. And it wasn't the skill of the bowler either. I was reading his bowling fine until the damned ball decided to get a mind of its own. You saw it, didn't you? It went backward, back up the wicket. You can't tell me that's natural, Carnacki."

On that, at least, I had to agree with him, for I could not deny what I had seen with my own eyes. But from what I knew of the Outer Darkness, I could not see what benefit was to be gained for any entity to come to this plane only to frustrate one particular team of middle-aged Sunday cricket players in a sleepy, English country village.

I did not mention this to Arkwright, of course. He would merely have taken it as evidence that even the Outer Darkness had an understanding of the serious nature and importance of the game of cricket. Instead, while Arkwright went to the bar, I studied the balls that had been used that day.

There was nothing untoward about any of them. If there was a presence here causing mischief, it was not doing it through the red leather of the balls. After that I looked at Arkwright's bat and leg pads, I even went so far as to study his cap, although I did not linger over that for the smell of hair cream and sweat was rather too heady.

Arkwright returned with another beer for each of us, and we talked for a while, about the recent history of the club, and whether there was any bad blood among any of the team members that might account for sabotage or trickery.

"There's the usual petty local politics that turn up in small town clubs," Arkwright agreed. "But there's nothing I can think of that would make anybody cause trouble out on the field of play. The game's too important for that kind of nonsense."

I waited while he fetched us both a last pint of beer from the bar.

"All this talk has indeed jogged my memory, Carnacki. There is one thing I've remembered," Arkwright said as he returned with the drinks. "Although it was last season, about this time, so it surely can't mean much of anything."

"And what was that?"

"We almost had a disaster. There was a bally great hole in the wicket, and it was right on the bowler's line. It was found in the morning before a match and it looked like a stone had fallen from the sky and embedded itself in the ground."

"A meteorite?"

"That's what Sergeant Wills said. He's no expert, but he's officialdom, if you see what I mean?"

"How big was this stone?"

"I prized it out with a trowel myself. It was no bigger than my thumb, but it felt heavier than it looked. As we didn't want any fuss, we got rid of the dashed thing, and rolled the wicket flat that same morning. It was just a bit of bother, and it was all over in a couple of minutes. I'm sure it didn't have anything to do with anything."

I, for my part however was not so sure of that. And it was the first indication I had that there might indeed be something to Arkwright's idea that this was in my area of expertise. I needed to have a closer look, and to pay more attention than I had been doing so far. I suggested we take a walk back over to the wicket for a closer look.

We headed outside and onto the field of play, where there was enough ambient light for us to make our way across to the wicket. I had Arkwright show me where the stone had fallen from the sky, passed him my glass, and got down on my hands and knees, patting at the turf, feeling for a cold spot, a presence, anything that might help me get to the bottom of Arkwright's problem.

But there was nothing of any note, just grass and dirt and a feeling that I was making myself look quite ridiculous. And my knees were damp from the gathering evening dew on the grass.

I stood, and we finished our beers there in the center of the field. All was silent in the cricket ground and the village beyond. A more peaceful and tranquil scene you will not find anywhere. If there was indeed an entity from the Outer Darkness present, it too was keeping quiet, perhaps even reveling in the tranquility.

I left to catch my train home without having been of much help to my friend at all.

★

My failure, as I saw it, preyed on my mind for much of the next week. I was spending the days at home, as I had put aside some time to study an obscure, dense, portion of the Sigsand mss, but my mind would not settle and kept returning to Arkwright's problem. I perused my library, looking for clues, searching for tales of meteorites and the magical effects thereof.

I already knew that the Oracle of Delphi was built around a stone from the sky, one that was said to have been regurgitated by Kronos. I also had some recollection of other, even older, tales in Babylonian myth and back, farther still, to cave drawings of our most distant ancestors that linked signs in the sky to high magic. I read tales of dark forces emanating from strange stones, of magic ritual summoning the power of the sky gods themselves, and of evil men wresting power from the rock. Of course I knew from my studies these were all merely facets of different views of the emanations from the Outer Darkness, and I now suspected some such to be at work on Arkwright's cricket wicket. But I could not for the life of me see how the trick with the bowlers might be accomplished.

After our dinner and story on the Friday, and, after ascertaining that Arkwright's team had another home match coming up, I asked him if I might be allowed to join them on the Sunday. He was only too happy to have me down to the ground again, although I think he was as unsure as I was myself whether I would be able to do anything to help the situation.

I traveled down on the early train on the Sunday morning, taking my box of defenses with me this time. I could not see a situation where I might be able to use them but I wanted them with me.

Just in case.

★

Arkwright was on the platform to meet me and helped carry the box of defenses the short distance down the lane to the cricket ground.

"I really hope you can help me out, old chap," he said. "We're still bottom of the bally league, and the season's half way over already."

"I'll do my best. This meteorite," I asked, "you said that you disposed of it. Can I see it? It might help if I had more of an idea as to what manner of rock it was."

Arkwright looked sheepish.

"I'm afraid I threw it in the bally river, old man," he said. "As far as I know, it's still down there with all the lost balls and sticklebacks."

But with that very thought, Arkwright had an idea.

"We do, however, have a small boat, and a fishing net. We pay a local lad tuppence for any balls he can fish out for us before they get too badly soaked to be of any use. We've got a few hours before the start of play. What do you say? Shall we go trawling?"

It was as good an idea as any one that I had, so after depositing my box of defenses in the clubhouse, we went out on the river. For the next few hours Arkwright rowed, enough to keep us from being carried away downstream, and I trawled along the riverbed with a long handled net.

We did indeed bring up several balls, all of which were too badly soaked to be of any use whatsoever. Alongside that we dredged up a variety of objects; there were old bottles, pieces of children's toys and the like. I studied any thumb-sized stones we brought up, but they were all too mundane, all too clearly local rock, and definitely of earthly origin.

We gave up when we spotted the opposition team arriving at the clubhouse for the afternoon's match.

★

Arkwright groaned loudly as he saw them.

"Damn it all. I'd forgotten it was the Sevenoaks chaps today. Their captain is a real blowhard, and he's no kind of gentleman at all. Worse than that he works upstairs from me in the office and has been taking great delight in our misfortunes of the season so far. I had hoped you might have this matter done and dusted before they came round, Carnacki, for if we lose to them today, I shall never hear the bally end of it."

As the teams warmed up before the match, I guessed at the man that Arkwright meant before having to have him pointed out, for he was a big, blustery chap with a booming voice and a personality to match. He ran his team like a dictator. He barked orders, and raged, red faced, if they weren't complied with immediately. I could already tell that he always took pains to ensure he was center of attention, and his braying voice was loud enough to frighten any small children in the vicinity. Even without Arkwright's earlier warning, I would have taken an immediate dislike to the man.

I went to the bar for a beer while the teams prepared for their tussle, then went back out into another warm, sunny afternoon as they took to the field. I found a seat, and sat with a pipe lit while Arkwright lost the toss. The big man from the Sevenoaks team laughed loudly, the sound carrying all around the field, although there was little humor in it. He elected to bat first and off we went.

★

The day went spectacularly wrong for poor Arkwright almost from the start. He opened the bowling against the big loud man. His first over went for twelve runs, his second for sixteen, and for the rest of their allocated bowling the Sevenoaks team's batsmen sent the ball fleeing to all parts of the ground. The big loud chap scored a century and they finally finished at a canter to a score of almost two hundred and fifty in their forty overs. Even I knew that was a total that was going to be dashed hard, if not impossible, for Arkwright's men to reach.

Arkwright's face was like thunder in the break between innings, so I kept my distance from him and sipped at my beer. There was only a small band of spectators, and none were inclined to engage me in conversation, so I contented myself with watching the chap with the big roller as he prepared the wicket before the local team went out to bat.

My old friend's day did not improve any when the Carlside team started their chase of the score. Arkwright faced up to the Sevenoaks' captain for the first delivery. It was a fast ball, but it looked like Arkwright had it covered. His bat was in line with the ball ready to strike, right up until the last second before impact. The ball hit the turf and went straight up in the air, arcing high over poor Arkwright's head to fall directly on top of the stumps, flattening all three of them. The Sevenoak's captain whooped and hollered in a most unsporting manner, and there were loud words spoken between him and Arkwright that, thankfully, were not audible to the watching crowd, as I fear it might have offended their delicate village sensibilities.

Arkwright's face was redder than the ball as he stomped off the pitch, and I soon heard a variety of things being thrown around in the room at my back. I thought it best not to go and investigate. I left him alone until his temper had worn off, and tried to concentrate on the match in front of me.

What followed in the next half an hour was the abject embarrassment of the Carlside team's batsmen. The ball had a life of its own, and was determined to get the batsmen out to even the mildest of deliveries; it bounced too high, too low, or took a turn at an impossible angle, all at the most inopportune moment for the batsmen. By the close of their innings, Carlside had managed a miserable thirty three runs between the lot of them, and the Sevenoaks captain could not contain his gloating glee when the last wicket fell giving them a winning margin of over two hundred runs.

It was a complete rout.

★

The Sevenoaks captain proved to be quite as graceless off the pitch as he had been on it, and gave a winner's speech full of gloating condescension. Arkwright, good sport to the last now that his temper had abated somewhat, clenched his teeth and shook the man's hand, but I could see there was little love lost between them.

My friend hardly said a word through an awkward supper and he did not come close to relaxing until the Sevenoaks men finally left, the Carlside team sloped off dejectedly homeward, and he and I were once again the sole occupants of the quiet bar.

"Dash it all, Carnacki, things cannot go on like this. I shall be a laughing stock in the office tomorrow as it is, and the rest of the lads in the team here don't deserve this kind of humiliation on a weekly basis. Some of them are even talking about chucking it in and taking up soccer, and that would be a real tragedy. Is there nothing you can do to help?"

As I was still at a loss to even define the nature of the problem, I did not see a course of action open to me, but Arkwright had asked for my help, and he needed something, so I thought I could at least give him a show. And maybe something might indeed reveal itself, if sufficiently provoked by the presence of the pentacle.

I had Arkwright move tables and chairs aside as I fetched my box, and I set up my defensive circles in the bar area before arranging the valves of the pentacle in the valleys and troughs of the points in the pentagram I drew inside them. I decided that, for once, it might be good to spend my vigil in a certain degree of comfort, so we placed two chairs inside the defenses, and also fetched ourselves some stiff measures of Scotch to keep us going should it be a long night.

Arkwright stepped inside the circles with me as the battery started to hum and the valves brightened sending washes of color around the bar. We had a clear view out of the open doorway to the wicket, and I kept a close eye on the flattened grass as the light started to go from the sky and a quiet dark fell over the cricket ground.

Then there was nothing to do but for us each to light a smoke and wait.

★

Unfortunately, waiting has never been Arkwright's strongest suit. He began fidgeting after only five minutes, and kept up a constant flow of chatter, mainly about the day's play. Like many enthusiasts of the game of cricket, he appeared to be able to memorize every ball bowled, every position taken by a fielder, and every shot played.

It was an impressive feat of mental gymnastics, I will admit that much, but I am afraid that I find it rather dull when taken to its extremes. Still, at least it kept his mind off anything that might end up being more sinister in nature for a while. I let him rattle on and smoked my pipe, keeping a close eye on the wicket outside and the shadows that gathered in the corners of the bar as the night grew darker and quieter.

Arkwright was banging on yet again about his own dismissal when I shushed him into silence. The yellow valve of my pentacle had brightened considerably, and outside, not on the wicket, but beyond that, over toward the river, an answering glow pulsed in the dark.

I drew Arkwright's attention to this latest phenomenon.

"What the blazes is it?" Arkwright whispered.

I took a bearing from where we were, and realized that the glow was indeed coming from where we had been on the boat earlier; it was emanating from somewhere out over the trout stream.

"I believe that we've found the location of your meteorite," I replied.

The yellow valve, and the glow out on the river, synchronized into a pulsing rhythm, a throb like a slow heartbeat. Washes of yellow filled the room around us. I waited to see if this would evolve into anything further, but the beat of the pulsing stayed slow and constant.

"Now what?" Arkwright whispered.

I looked around. There had to be something else, something nearer than the river that could have the effects on the balls bowled that I'd seen earlier. But the wicket area itself still sat in dark shadows and there was no sign of a glow there.

It was as I looked away that I caught a glimmer in a deeper area of shadow, faint at first, but as my eyes adjusted and focused I saw it plain enough. Something, a very small, almost imperceptible something, glowed and pulsed in time with the yellow of my valve and the meteorite outside. And whatever it was, it was outside the door of the bar.

But to investigate further, I would have to step out of the defenses.

★

I was loath to open myself to any kind of attack, but Arkwright had no such qualms, and he too had seen the same glimmer of yellow that had caught my attention. Before I could stop him he got up from his chair, stepped out of the circles and headed for the doorway. At least he'd had the sense not to smudge the chalked circles, but his impetuosity was, to my mind, reckless in the extreme.

"Get back in here, man," I said. "We don't know what we're dealing with yet."

Arkwright didn't stop, but at least he answered me.

"A bally nuisance, that's what we're dealing with," he replied. "And I've had about enough of it."

He went out the door and out of my sight. Everything fell quiet and still.

"Arkwright?"

I got no answer this time. My fear for my friend was stronger than my worry about leaving the defenses. I rose and went outside. My heart was in my mouth, and I feared the worst, but I found him crouched over something. He moved aside to give me room and I saw that it was the heavy roller I had seen the chap use on the wicket before the strange behavior of the ball.

Arkwright pointed at a spot where a faint yellow glow, like the light of a firefly, pulsed and faded in time with the larger glow out on the river and the yellow valve of my pentacle in the room behind us. We bent closer, and as my eyes adjusted to the gloom I got a better look at the source of the yellow.

There was something embedded in the roller, almost miniscule, a tiny yellow fleck of stone. Arkwright tried to cut it free with his penknife but although it was small, it was deeply embedded and buried too deep to be got out.

"That's our blasted culprit, isn't it, Carnacki?" he asked in a hushed voice.

On careful consideration, I had to agree with his diagnosis. I had seen the roller being used for myself, and had seen the effect on the balls bowled shortly afterward, not just today, but in the previous match the week before too.

I could not explain it, but I didn't have to, for Arkwright was happier now that he had something to focus on.

"Well done, Carnacki," he said, smiled and clapped me on the shoulder. "You've found the blasted nuisance right enough. I shall take it from here."

"But this thing must be investigated," I replied. "And we must be careful to dispose of it properly."

"Oh, don't worry yourself about that, old man," Arkwright replied. "I'll see that everything ends up exactly where it is supposed to."

★

And that was the end of my adventure at the cricket club. The yellow glow on the roller, and the one out on the river, faded as soon as I switched off the pentacle and was gone completely by the time all of my kit was back in the box. While I was clearing up, Arkwright had taken a line of sight and made a drawing so that he could take the rowing boat over to the right place in the daylight and retrieve the original fallen stone.

We shook hands on the station platform as the last train of the night came in to take me back up to town.

"Do not go doing anything rash," I said to him as we parted. "I have your word that you will dispose of everything properly? I'd suggest burying it deep in sold rock somewhere remote."

Arkwright smiled.

"I told you, old man, I'll see it gets to where it needs to go, I promise."

I never did find out whether he kept his word but I suspect his idea of disposing of it properly and mine might be at odds with each other, given what I learned at our next meeting.

He took me aside before dinner this last Friday.

"I did as you requested, Carnacki. I got rid of both sources of the yellow glow."

"Did you get dispose of them in the right place?" I asked.

He smiled, winked, and changed the subject.

He then told me, proudly, that they'd played an away

game on the Sunday, in Sevenoaks. The home team had a minor problem with their pitch, but it had been fixed in time for the game to go ahead.

"I got a hundred with the bat and we put on nearly three hundred. They got their new heavy roller out on the field after that," he said. "Those blighters were out for less than fifty. You should have seen it, Carnacki. I bowled that bounder, their captain, first ball, with one that took two different sharp turns on the way into the stumps."

The King's Treasure

I was late in arriving at Cheyne Walk that autumn evening, held behind at work by an important document for an even more important client that could not wait until Monday. I did not take time to return home to change out of my working suit, but even so it was a full ten minutes past the hour by the time I arrived on Carnacki's doorstep.

So it was that almost as soon as Carnacki took my coat, we were all led through to the dining room where the first course was already laid out and waiting. Fortunately it was a cold salad of succulent smoked mackerel and berries so I had not been the cause of anyone's supper going cold. The main course was a haunch of dashed fine roast venison with potatoes and buttered cabbage, washed down with a pint of strong brown ale and excellent company. The chaps were all in fine form, and I had quite forgotten my tardiness and frustration by the time we settled in the parlor with our glasses charged and our smokes lit.

Carnacki started into his latest story without further ado.

★

"I have long since ceased to be surprised by the frequency in which my path has crossed with that of Gault, the ship's captain that I have shared adventures with on several occasions these recent years. You will, of course, remember that the chap is an inveterate rogue, although one with a considerable amount of charisma and charm, two qualities that can often combine to get him into sticky situations.

"Tonight's tale involves one such situation, and once again it begins with the captain requesting my help in a matter that would prove to be only just on the right side of legality."

★

"It began twelve days ago, on the Monday morning. I was up town in the Strand doing some business when I heard my name being called from across the street, and when I looked up, who should I see but our captain, waving frantically and trying to catch my eye. I crossed the road to meet him when the traffic allowed, where he met me with a smile and pumped my hand with an iron grip that belied the salt and pepper in his voluminous beard.

"Carnacki, by all that is holy, it is indeed you. Well met, indeed, my friend. This is truly a fortuitous meeting. Are you too busy to join me for a spot of lunch?"

He gave me every impression that we had happened to bump into each other that morning. But if I had any thought that this was merely a chance meeting, the notion was dispelled immediately we started to chat over ale and a pie in *The George* ten minutes later.

"'I already tried you at home this morning,' Gault admitted straight off, for although he had plenty of native guile and could have easily lied to my face, I think he did indeed see me as more of a friend than a business opportunity. 'Your neighbor at four-seventy, Mr. Brown, told me that you were up town on business, and he also told me where to look for you.'

"I made a mental note to henceforth refrain from sharing my personal matters with Brown next door, then I had to pay attention as Gault eventually got to the point of our now obviously far from impromptu meeting.

"'I have grave need of your specialist skills again, Carnacki,' he said. 'There is a small, and delicate, problem that only you can help with. I think I can promise to make it well worth your while though. If the salvage is done right, there's a King's ransom to be made in it.'

"He chuckled at that, as if he had made a fine joke, but he was not about to explain the nature of it. Instead, he was now studying me, as if waiting for my agreement. That was something I was loath to do on such little information.

"'You are undertaking another salvage operation?' I asked. 'You almost lost an arm the last time, remember? And how can I possibly help with salvage? It is your line of expertise, not mine.'

"Gault supped long and deep on his ale, then leaned close to me, his voice low when he replied.

"'Well, you see, Carnacki, it's not exactly the recovery

itself I need help with; I need you to lift the bloody curse that's on the thing I'm trying to salvage.'

★

"I had been on the verge of thanking him for the ale and leaving, but that last sentence stopped me in my tracks, and I stayed in my chair listening as he laid out his problem.

"'I got the nod that there was something found by a fisherman off the East Coast of Scotland a month or so back. It was part of a tale told by a lad in his cups in a Whitby bar. Now, normally I discount such things, but this one had a ring of truth in it, for me at least, and you already know I've got a nose for a good bit of business when it comes my way.

"'So the very next morning, I upped anchor from Whitby and headed north at full steam. I've had *The Mary Anne* sitting off Burntisland in Fife these past three weeks,' he said. 'Being a historian and a scholar yourself, you know the import of the place's name, and what lies in the water offshore I presume?'

"I did indeed know the story, as I guess all of you chaps here do too. What schoolboy has not had his heart beating faster at the thought of a King's treasure to be found on a Scottish seabed in shallow waters?

"'You are after the Charles the First's barge, *The Blessing of Burntisland,* aren't you?' I said. "The one that went down in rough seas in 1633 with his treasure on board?'

"Gault smiled.

"'It was not exactly a difficult conclusion to come to, was it? The story is known well enough, after all. And it is spoken of in hushed tones wherever old pirates like me gather for business; the lure of the silver dinner service alone would have been enough for me to pay attention, never mind the other reported wealth the retinue was carrying when it was lost.'

"'No, you're right,' I replied. 'It was not a great leap of deduction on my part. But that ferry went down in rough waters nearly three centuries ago. Tide and current will surely have strewn it far and wide by now? The fact it has never been found is surely no coincidence. Far better men than you have wasted their lives looking for it."

"'They did not have my advantage,' Gault replied. 'I have the tale of the fisherman in Whitby, who spoke of finding two silver spoons in his nets, and told me the exact location where he was at the time by line of sight with two lighthouses and Burntisland itself. I have also acquired access to the very latest in diving equipment, and a pretty penny it cost me too. And in a way, the new kit is why I need your help.'

"I will admit it, I was starting to become bally intrigued, despite my misgivings about any involvement with the loveable rogue again. But I still needed more information before I would be willing to commit myself to his cause.

"'You said something about a curse?'

"'Aye,' Gault replied. 'Every time we try to make a dive. I've got blasted air giving out, lines getting fouled, anchors not taking grip on the sea bed, and suits springing mystery leaks; any one of them I'd be able to shrug off as a minor problem, but all of the at once? It's too much to be mere happenstance.'

"'And you have definitely ruled out sabotage?'

"He nodded, and looked grim as he supped again at his ale.

"'These are hand-picked men this time, Carnacki. I've crewed with them all in some damned rough ports and rougher storms. I'd trust them all with my mother's life. No, I've got a hunch that I am right on this one. This is definitely in your line of work.'

"And you know what? I had to agree, for I knew something that Gault did not about the vessel he was attempting to raise. It was something hinted at in a book I had read years before, and I still had the same tome in my library in Chelsea. When I told this to Gault, he decided he had to see it forthwith, and by that time I most definitely had the scent of an adventure in my nostrils and so was quite happy to oblige him."

★

"An hour later we were back here in Chelsea, drinking my scotch, smoking my cheroots, and looking over the book I'd taken down from the shelf. It was handwritten rather than printed, and more in the nature of a journal than a book.

Purportedly, it had been written after the tragedy that befell the King's Barge. The language was in broader Scots than either of us were used to, but we got the gist of it well enough.

"The writer was one Alexander Seton, an alchemist, some say sorcerer, of some note in the annuls of Scotland's occult history. I have several of his journals and notebooks in my library, for his field of study has several overlaps with my own. This particular entry was dated the year of the barge's sinking, and he had been there, on a boat behind the very vessel that Gault was now seeking on the seabed.

★

"'*I telt the King's man he should be more circumspect, that there was something brooding in the waters beyond Burntisland that was best avoided, but he widna listen to me. I was telt that the King's treasure had to get to Edinburgh by the fastest route possible, a show of wealth for the London parliament to take note of. Politics and nonsense is all that it was, and it damned near got us all killed, for politicians and kings are not the only things on land or sea to covet shining silver and gold trinkets.*

"'*I hae long kent there is something down there. The monks of Lindisfarne mention it in their manuscripts, and there are dark mutterings in Roman scrolls in the Vatican, stories about an eater of boats in the Forth. But as I hae said, the King's man widna listen. And now he is deid, along with a hunner others.*

"*They were twa hunner yairds ahead of us when it happened, and all that we saw was a boiling froth of water unner the ferry before it went down. But I felt it. I felt it in my bones and in my water. It is a dark thing, huge and black and formless, and it is hungry, as hungry for gold as any King.*

"'*I hae telt the new King's man to keep his boats well away from the spot.*

Mayhap this wan will listen tae me.'"

★

"'I was right, then?' Gault said when I closed the book. 'This is definitely in your line of expertise?'

"'It certainly appears so,' I replied. 'Although on reading

WILLIAM MEIKLE | 89

that, I am not so sure you would not be best served by leaving things well enough alone.'

"Then he told me how much money he thought was involved, and I knew why he would not be taking a backward step unless it was absolutely necessary. The figure he quoted to me would, I believe, pay for the running of the whole country for a good few months, if not an entire year.

"There was another factor at play too; our good captain had already sunk most of what he owned into the venture, and he owed the banks a bit more on top of that, so he would not listen to any of my protestations.

"Besides, I will admit that the whole bally thing intrigued me and had me more than a tad curious. I had always written old Seton's tale off as another Highlander's sea monster story but the fact that there might be something to it meant that I would have to go and see for myself.

"So it was that Gault and I made our way by carriage to Kings Cross Railway Station that very afternoon, and thence to points north. I took my larger box of defenses with me. I had a feeling they might be needed."

★

"Gault proved to be a most amiable companion on the train journey to Edinburgh, keeping me regaled with tales of skullduggery and adventure on the high seas in remote climes. He has a distinctive way with a story. Indeed, if I ever get the chance, I shall invite him to one of our evenings, and you can enjoy his company for yourselves.

"We partook of afternoon tea on the train, and what with that, and a couple of stiff brandies in the dining carriage, the trip was as comfortable as such a journey could ever be.

"The remainder of our journey after changing trains in Edinburgh was, unfortunately, rather less pleasant. It was a filthy evening, of the kind that only Scotland seems to be able to provide. The rain lashed hard against the carriage windows, and a snell wind whistled through the train.

"I felt damp and cold even before we came to a halt. When we finally disembarked from the rickety, rattling carriage in Burntisland, we had to carry our luggage, and my box of defenses, in the dark, down across an exposed shoreline to the pier where Gault had a rowboat moored up. Out beyond the moorings I saw nothing but more rain, a heavy swell, and a pitch-black darkness from horizon to horizon. If there was a boat out there, I could not see it.

"I complained long and bitterly about taking to the sea in such conditions, but Gault merely laughed at my soft landlubber ways. He was already down in the rowboat, and looking up at me expectantly.

"'This? This is nothing but a drop of rain, man. Get aboard. We'll be aboard in ten minutes and you'll be fine after some coffee and scotch.'

"I finally relented and joined him in the small rowboat, which, to my surprise, was quite sturdy and seaworthy and barely rocked or rolled even when we left the harbor and headed into the blackness beyond.

"To his credit, Gault was as good as his word, although I do believe the ten minutes he spent rowing us out to *The Mary Anne* might have been the most miserable of my life, for although the swell was just about manageable, the rain did not relent. By the time his men helped us aboard, I was soaked all the way through my suit to my skin and feeling more than a little delicate in the gut.

"A change of clothes, a plate of hot stew, a coffee and two glasses of his fine scotch did much to revive me. By the time I felt ready to try a pipe I finally had time to consider the scale of his operation out here in the open Firth.

"*The Mary Anne* was an old schooner, a three master that had been converted to steam, with a wide handsome upper deck belying the rather cramped quarters below.

"'She was built a few miles up the coast,' Gault informed me. 'She's a local lassie, from Dundee, although she's seen the world since then. I got her for a song from a chap in the Carib who was down on his luck, but before that she saw service from the Antarctic all the way to the Baltic, as a scientific vessel and then little more than a coal trawler. She can handle all weathers, and as much cargo as we can cram into her.'

"He spoke lovingly, as if describing a sweetheart, which, in a sense, I suppose she was."

★

"I sat in the wheel house with Gault while his crew scurried to and fro in the rain, making sure everything was secure as the wind got up a notch and we started to roll and sway. This did not do my delicate stomach that much good, and Gault laughed at my obvious discomfort.

"'Give it an hour, man,' he said. 'You'll see, you'll find your sea legs soon enough.'

"Surprisingly, he was right, for after more scotch and another smoke, I started to feel almost normal, although I do not think I shall ever prefer the deck of a boat at sea to the feel of solid ground underfoot.

"By this time the crew had all retired to drier quarters below decks. Gault and I shared drinks from his whisky bottle. We played chess, on a fine scrimshaw set with pieces that splendidly depicted whales, dolphins and other cetaceans, and we smoked some of his rather acrid, dark, pipe tobacco while the rain lashed ever harder on the windows of the wheel house.

"Gault proved to be a fine player, with a quick style of play and an attacking flair I was hard pushed to defend against. I was considering a risky, but potentially game-winning move, when Gaunt went still and quiet, and a strange hush fell around us. I was about to speak when he put a finger to his lips, and mouthed a single word.

"'Listen'

"I did as requested, and at first I only heard the rain. Then it came to me, distant and faint, like a massed choir singing in the wind, a chorus of voices raised in a hymn. The words were clear enough, although they made little sense to me at the time.

"'*She sleeps in the deep, with the fish far below,*'
"'*She sleeps, in the deep, in the dark,*'
"'*She sleeps, and she dreams, in the deep, in the deep,*'
"'*And the Dreaming God is singing here she lies.*'"

"The wind rose again, and the song faded away, until it was as if it had never been there. I looked over at Gaunt and he smiled grimly.

"'Yes, Carnacki. It was all too real. I heard it too. We all hear it. It comes mostly at night, and mostly in the wind. The crew says it is the spirits of the King's dead barge crew, lost in the deep, down in the cold dark, calling us down to join them. And I am not sure as I disagree with them on that score.

"'It is all I can do to keep the men here at all. And some nights, nights much like this one, I'm of a mind to turn tail and flee with them.'

"'So what keeps you here in this foul weather?'

"'It is not always like this. You'll see for yourself in the morning. And the money, man; think of the money!'

"He checkmated me some five minutes later, for I had quite lost my concentration and enthusiasm for the game. It was not the money I was thinking of when I finally found my way to the small cabin I had been allocated. I climbed into the bunk with my head almost up against the outside keel, and as I drifted into a fitful sleep, it was as if I heard the chorus again, faint and distant, but most insistent.

"'*Where she lies, where she lies, where she lies, where she lies,*'
"'*The Dreaming God is singing where she lies.*'"

★

"Gault had been right about one thing; the weather was markedly improved in the morning. I woke to bright sunlight streaming in the porthole above my bunk, and any apprehension I had been feeling after hearing the singing in the night was quite washed away by the loud cawing of the herring gulls and the soft lap of wavelets on the outer hull.

"I made what ablutions I could manage in the cramped conditions of the cabin and then went up on deck. Gaunt was already in the wheelhouse, and had a pot of coffee on the go. I took to it gratefully. It was strong and black and tasted exactly how I needed it to taste to get my morning going with a jolt to the system. Indeed, I was starting to feel at home, and felt even more so when the ship's cook arrived with a plate of eggs, ham and toast that looked large enough to fortify me for the rest of the day.

"The crew were already hard at work on the main deck. When I finished my breakfast and went out for a smoke I could see they were making preparations for a dive.

"Two of the men had already climbed into heavy

rubberized suits and were being helped in affixing the large copper helmets and air tubes. The tubes themselves were attached to large pumps on the fore-deck that were hooked up to a generator to keep air circulating even when the divers were at some depth.

"'How deep do they have to go?' I asked as Gault came to my side.

"'The seabed's about a hundred feet below us here, no more,' he replied. 'The suits can handle twice that, or so the German manufacturers tell me. You asked about my advantage yesterday? Well there it is, Carnacki; we have at our disposal the finest diving equipment that money can buy. I am hoping that with these new suits, and your expertise, we can get this job underway properly from today onwards, be over and done with it quickly, and back to the gaudy lights of London together to enjoy the spoils.'

"I was still rather unsure as to what help I might be, but I held my peace and watched the divers complete their preparations. I saw tension in the captain before the dives started, and worry for the fate of his men. He chewed on the stem of his pipe hard enough to leave the impression of his teeth on the ebony. As the men went down into the water in their cages and the chains clattered and clacked, I realized his tension was contagious; I felt my heart leap and flutter, as if it were I and not the crewmen who were heading down, all alone, into the cold dark.

"And the damnable thing about it was that there was nothing we could do; there was no choice but to wait and see what transpired. I had some more of Gault's rough tobacco, and more of his almost as rough coffee, and the minutes passed ever so slowly while we waited.

"Finally the chains stopped clattering, and there was only the thud and thump of the pumps to be heard.

"The men were on the bottom."

★

Carnacki paused there. He has an almost preternatural knack of knowing the exact point to leave a story to build the maximum amount of tension, and no little frustration, in his audience. Arkwright in particular seemed fit to burst, and hurried to refill his glass with brandy and get a fresh smoke lit.

"Dash it man, hurry yourself up," he said as Carnacki smiled and, deliberately I thought, took his sweet good time in lighting his pipe.

Finally, with our host puffing happily, we were all ready again, and he took up the tale where he had left off.

★

"The next five minutes were jolly hard on our captain.

"'Is this an especially fraught moment?' I asked, realizing even as I said it how naïve a question it was when two men were so many feet of water away below us in the cold, silent, dark. But if Gault took any umbrage, he was too good a chap to show it.

"'If anything is to go wrong, it will be about now,' was all he would say, then he chewed so hard on his pipe I thought he might break it in two pieces.

"The pumps kept up their solid thumping, and after an age, the chains started to clank and rattle once more. I'm not a seafaring man, but even I knew what that signified.

"The men were coming up.

"I thought I could discern more strain on the cables and chains on the ascent. Gault patrolled the deck, barking orders and ensuring the raising of the cages would be as smooth as they could manage, but it still took an interminable time and the strain on the cables had them screeching and wailing all the way up.

"We saw the reason why when the cages were finally raised up onto the deck. The divers waved and gave thumbs-up to indicate that they had returned safely in one piece. More than that, it was soon apparent that they had brought with them what appeared to be a King's ransom in treasure.

"There was silver plate, tarnished of course after its stay on the sea bed, a stout wooden chest, only partially rotted, filled to the brim with gold pieces, and a stiff burlap sack that, when emptied proved to be full of jewel-studded bracelets, necklaces and headpieces of obvious antiquity.

"Gault grinned, and clasped me on the shoulders.

"'You're our lucky charm, man.'

"'He certainly is, Cap'n,' one of the divers said as he was helped off with his helmet. 'For there's more where that came from; there's a damned sight more. It's murky and dark and cold all right, but the stuff's lying on the bottom waiting to be brought up.'"

★

I sat in the wheelhouse, drinking too much coffee and smoking Gault's rough tobacco while the salvage team went into full operation through the morning and early afternoon. The sound of the great pumps thudded and echoed across the water and reverberated all through the hull. I felt every beat in the soles of my shoes, and it pounded, like incessant drumming, in my head. What with that, and the clatter of chains, the shouts of the crew and the screeching of excited gulls, it was all one bally long commotion that gave me quite a headache and had me wishing for the peace and quiet of my little library back here in Chelsea.

The only saving grace was the excitement brought on every time a fresh load of items was delivered up from below, the anticipation of which had us all behaving like children anticipating a present. By the time the sun started to sink over the rolling hills of Fife, the deck was covered in a bewildering array of wondrous items. Some of it was treasure, some was little more than rotted garments that had once graced a King's fine wardrobe but were now home to colonies of barnacle, crab and weed. But all of it was almost spellbinding in what it showed us of the history that had lain on the seabed all these long years.

"Gault had most of the crew working full stop on cleaning up anything that was thought to be of value. He showed me a leaded crystal goblet on a wrought silver base that he estimated was worth over a hundred guineas on its own, and he was clearly delighted with the fruits of the day's labor.

"The last dive was still on the bottom as the final red-gold rays of the sun kissed the keel of the boat and the sky darkened quickly from the east. Despite the riches strewn on the deck, I sensed a growing apprehension in the crew, and the steady thump of the pumps developed a stammering stutter, almost failed then started up again. But the steady rhythm we'd been keeping all day had been broken, and Gault caught the change in mood.

"'Fetch them back up, right now,' he called out. 'We've had a good enough day so far, there's no need to spoil it by over reaching ourselves. We'll get at it again first thing in the morning; it'll still be down there waiting for us. It's not going anywhere, and neither are we.'

"As for myself, I too was now taken by a growing foreboding, a sense that something was coming, a pricking of my thumbs if you like. I went so far as to fetch my box of defenses from the cabin, and opened it up in the bridge, preparing should the need arise to move swiftly.

"The process of bringing up the divers was still ongoing, and took an age. Darkness was falling fast, and the lights of the mainland were twinkling bright against the dark hills beyond. The gulls had abandoned us now, shadowy and fleeting as they made their way off to their nightly roosting spots. The only sound was from the machinery on the deck. The generator whined as the pumps thudded and chains rattled. It no longer felt smooth and effortless. The equipment shuddered, sending vibrations running through *The Mary Anne* that shook me to my bones and rattled my teeth.

"By this time, our captain had quite forgotten his earlier smiles and was marching about the deck barking orders with a grim set to his features.

"'Fetch them up,' he shouted again although it was obvious that the cables were being brought back in as fast as the machinery could pull them. The last hint of red left the western sky and it was almost full dark by the time the cages showed at the water line and were swung up over the gunwales and onto the deck. And this time, despite the strain we'd all noted on the chains and winches, there was only the two, fully suited, divers, with no sign that they had brought any further treasures back with them from the sea floor.

"The suited men stood stock still, unnaturally so in my opinion, and the sea air took on a sudden chill that had not been apparent seconds earlier. Damp, cold, air washed through the vessel like a wave, and I smelled the stench of rot and decay in my nose and at the back of my throat, stronger even than Gault's rough tobacco. My feeling of foreboding grew almost too strong to ignore.

"'Get them out of that gear,' I shouted.

"One of the helmeted divers turned towards the sound. All I saw in the visor was darkness, and a swirling, deep-green flow that looked like the depths of the ocean.

"'You heard the man,' Gault added. 'Look lively, lads.'

One of the crew finally went to obey the captain's order, and stepped forward, reaching up as if to help remove the nearest diver's helmet from the suit. The diver finally moved, and threw out an arm as rigid as iron that struck the crewman in the chest. The poor, startled, chap flew, a good three yards across the deck to land with a crash in a pile of silver plate.

"'Gault,' I shouted. 'Keep your men back. This is in my domain now.'

"The helmeted figure turned at the shout. I saw only a shifting flow of what appeared to be green fluid behind the visor, and now I was sure of what I was seeing. There wasn't a man in there at all, or if there was he had been completely subsumed. What I was seeing was something of the Outer Darkness, something that had been sleeping in the cold dark; something that was now all too obviously awake."

★

"I moved quickly to fetch my box of defenses out onto the deck and had Gault and his men clear a space for me. The suited divers, or whatever things inhabited them, were moving sluggishly around, as if unsure of their surroundings. Several of Gault's men had already armed themselves with billhooks and iron bars and looked ready to set upon any attack if one came. But I had no time to observe; I knew that I had to get a defensive circle in place right smartish, before some God-awful doom descended and sent us all to the bottom to join the King's men already sleeping there.

"Even as I drew out the first circle in chalk, I heard the chanting rise in the air again, as distant as before, and still sounding like a choir singing against a wind. I turned my head, trying to pinpoint a source for the sound, but it appeared, impossibly, to be coming from every direction at once. The words were the same verse as I had heard the night before.

"*'She sleeps in the deep, with the fish far below,'*
"*'She sleeps, in the deep, in the dark,'*

"The rubber suited figures stopped moving, heads raised and cocked to one side, looking for all the world as if they were listening to the chanting. The green flowing fluid behind their visors surged and swirled ever faster as the voices grew louder.

"*'She sleeps, and she dreams, in the deep, in the deep,'*
"*'And the Dreaming God is singing here she lies.'"*

"By the time I finished the second of my outer circles, the divers were moving more purposefully, and they headed directly for the large mound of silver plate that sat pied high on the deck. Gault's men were not about to give up their share of the treasure lightly though. Two burly chaps, real bruisers that you wouldn't want to meet in a dark alley, moved to stand between the divers and the silver, blocking their path.

"The suited divers went through them as if they were nothing but children. A stiff arm caught one sailor in the chest and tossed him aside in a flailing rush of arms and legs to land hard on the deck. He stayed down and I saw that one of his legs was bent at a most unusual angle, broken in at least two places. The other sailor took a hammer blow to the head that felled him at the diver's feet in a heap like a broken doll.

"By this time I was laying out the pentacle and missed some of the next minute or so of action, but I heard it well enough. Cries of anger turned to wails of pain, there were loud cracks of heads hitting the deck and, above it all, the distant, but now louder, sound of the chanting.

"*'Where she lies, where she lies, where she lies, where she lies,'*

"By the time I had everything hooked up and switched on the valves, half a dozen of Gault's crew were strewn about, and the two divers, ignoring the wails and moans of the injured, had begun tossing the silver plate overboard.

"The valves blazed into life, sending rainbow washes of color across the deck, the hum as they brightened almost, but not quite, obscuring the sound of the chanting. I stepped into the circles. Three of Gault's men caught the gist immediately and stepped in beside me, but Gault was aghast at seeing his new found treasure, and his prospects of fame and fortune, being so wantonly tossed back into the deep. He now had a long-barreled pistol in one hand, and the crystal goblet he had shown to me earlier in the other.

"'By all that is holy,' he shouted. 'I will not let you take my prize so easily; not when I am so close.'

"I knew he was about to make a great mistake, but I did not have time to stop him. My shout was caught in my throat at the sound of his pistol shot. It hit the nearest diver full in the visor. The glass shattered, and darkness flowed out from the new hole, a green, fluid, darkness that washed across the decks as if alive.

"Gault was so astonished that he appeared to be rooted to the spot. I called for him, but he didn't hear me, so I did the only thing I could. I stepped out of the protections and ran across the deck, heading for the captain even as the green dark fluid surged and sent a wave toward the pair of us."

★

"I felt cold and dark and deep grip at me. The chanting appeared to rise to a crescendo. I heard it echo and boom, as if a thousand voices were singing inside my head.

"'*The Dreaming God is singing where she lies.*'

"Somehow I forced myself forward until I was within reach of the captain, and I stretched out a hand. It felt like I moved through thick molasses, but finally my fingertips met the material of his coat and it was as if a spell had been broken and I could move more freely. I grabbed his shoulder, and Gault came to his senses.

"Even then he tried to raise the pistol. I saw that he meant to shoot the other suited diver, but I knew there was no time for that. I dragged Gault backward, headed for the pentacle, and was able to get him to step over the drawn chalk circles before the wave of green washed against the defenses.

"I winced, expecting the circle, the pentacle, and perhaps even all of us left standing, to be washed away, but to my amazement the defenses held. The green darkness splashed against the outer circle, then hissed and boiled, turning to a misty steam that hung around the outside edge past the crystal valves. The valves themselves pulsed in time with the rhythm of the chanting, green, then blue, then yellow brightening and fading in turn as wave after wave of the swirling fluid broke against the circles and was repelled.

"It appeared we were safe, for now. But we were far from being out of danger.

"The green fluid washed forward and back across the deck, covering the whole surface from where we stood right up to the bow, traveling in a wave some three feet high. And where it passed, nothing was left behind it. Fallen men, machinery, and all of the piles of the captain's treasure were all washed away overboard. We heard it go, clattering and splashing over the sides, and felt the boat rock and sway under us as if taken in a heavy swell. The singing continued to echo around us, from everywhere and nowhere, more voices joined in song now, a great multitude of them.

"'*She sleeps in the deep, with the fish far below,*'
"'*She sleeps, in the deep, in the dark,*'

"There was one, last, surge, of green black water and I tasted salt spray at my lips, smelled rot and decay in my nose and throat. The valves of the pentacle all flared brightly at the same time, gleaming like small suns in the dark, then the boat stopped rocking, the choir stopped singing, and everything fell still and went quiet.

"The wave of green was gone, and the deck was clear of everything, everything except for the five of us standing in the pentacle, and the remaining rubber suited figure of the second diver."

★

"Gault was at my shoulder, looking out over the barren deck. Even the heavy housing of the pumps had been washed away, leaving only torn decking and bent gunwales to show it had ever been there, and there was not a single scrap of his treasure left save what he had in his hand. He still held the same crystal goblet with the silver base he had shown me earlier, the only remnant left of everything that had been brought up from below. He clutched it tight to his chest with his left hand as the rubber suited figure turned to face us.

"Once again we all saw a wash of green fluid stir and swirl behind the visor. The blue valve of the pentacle pulsed in time with the heavy, weighted, footsteps on the deck as the diver came towards us.

"Gault raised the pistol in his right hand and aimed directly at the approaching figure.

"'Don't be daft, man,' I said. 'Don't you remember the last time you did something that stupid?'

"At first I thought he would take no heed of me, for his dander was well and truly up but then I saw his gaze soften, the rage ebbing away, and he nodded, lowering the weapon as the diver approached the outer circle of the defenses.

"The blue valve whined and blazed as the figure tried to step forward, but it could not penetrate the circle. It tried again, and again the blue valve flared, and held firm.

"'It appears we are at an impasse,' Gault said sardonically.

"The diver stood still but I got the impression, do not ask me how I knew, that there was something of some intelligence inside that damned suit. And even now it was calculating its advantage. But Gault was right; we were at somewhat of an impasse. We were all safe, for the time being, inside the circle, but with the suited diver, and the green darkness inside it, patrolling outside the defenses.

"'What now, Carnacki?' Gault asked, and I realized that he was looking to me for an answer. I saw that the remaining crewmen, despite being in somewhat of a funk, were waiting to hear my response.

"'We might manage to last out the night, if my battery holds its charge long enough,' I replied. 'I suggest we stay in the defenses and wait it out.'

"But as it turned out, we were not to be given the opportunity to try. The green inside the diver's visor swirled and surged and the far off singing started up again.

"'*She sleeps in the deep, with the fish far below.*'

"'*She sleeps in the deep, in the dark,*'

"The sea started to roil and bubble in a wide patch all around us, and *The Mary Anne* once more bucked and rolled, so much so that we were almost thrown off our feet and out of the pentacle entirely. Gault in particular had to be nimble on his toes to avoid stepping on the defenses' chalk lines.

"The old boat's timbers creaked alarmingly. Huge waves, seawater, not green darkness this time, sloshed across the forward half of the bow.

"'If we have a wave like that hit us here, we can say goodbye to the defenses,' I said.

"The front of the vessel went up alarmingly, then back down again, hard, with a splash and a shock that once again nearly sent us tumbling.

"'What more do you want from me!' Gault shouted into the darkness.

"The rubber suited diver stood outside the outer circle and put out a hand. I knew immediately what was needed.

"'Give it the goblet, man.'

"'I will not, Gault replied. 'I must salvage something from this debacle.'

"The boat rocked from side to side, almost turning over completely and the water seethed as if in a turmoil driven from below. The unseen choir bellowed.

"'Where she lies, where she lies, where she lies, where she lies,'

"'Give it the blasted goblet, man, before we all go to join the men of the King's barge.'

'Somewhere on the boat a timber cracked, louder than the noise Gault's pistol had made earlier, and *The Mary Sue* took on a definite port-side list.

"'We're taking in water, Cap'n,' one of the crewmen said, and that, more than anything else, enabled Gault to make up his mind. He stepped forward and, with the pistol aimed at the diver's body, handed over the goblet.

"The figure took it in its left hand and bent stiffly at the waist, as if bowing in acknowledgement. Then it turned away. It walked to the gunwale and went over head first, hitting the water with a loud splash. That was the signal for whatever storm had gripped us to abate as quickly as it had come. The sea fell still, the rocking ceased, although we still listed alarmingly to port, and the chanting diminished and faded until there was only the last line, echoing across the waters.

"'*The Dreaming God is singing where she lies.*'"

★

Carnacki stopped, his tale almost done.

"There is not much left to tell. We had enough crew remaining to ensure that the bally boat didn't sink, and Gault managed to get us underway enough to limp into Burntisland the next morning. After a breakfast where nobody had much to say, I took my leave, making a long, slow way home with my box of tricks and my luggage.

"As for Gault, he says he is down to his last penny, but that is a tale I have heard from him before and he has always come back from the brink. I have no doubt that I, and you chaps too, will be hearing again from our captain."

He ushered us to the door.

"Now, out you go."

MR. CHURCHILL'S SURPRISE

From the personal journal of Thomas Carnacki, 472 Cheyne Walk, Chelsea.

As I have mentioned elsewhere in these journals, there are several of my cases I cannot relate to Dodgson and the others at all. Some of them involve maintaining a degree of delicacy and decorum. For example, there is a great Lady of the land who would be most embarrassed should details of her involuntary nocturnal wanderings ever become public.

But there are other cases, often dark, often furtive, that I must by rights keep close to my chest. This is not because they are too alarming or disturbing for my good friends, but purely because if I did tell anyone, I would in all probability meet my end in a dark cell on bread and water for the rest of my natural life. That is, if I did not see the end of a hangman's rope first. Matters of national security are tricky things at the best of times, and when they call for my peculiar area of expertise, they tend to become even more peculiar still and even less available for public consumption.

My friend, Dodgson has written elsewhere of my infrequent encounters with the extraordinary Mr. Winston Churchill, and the matter I will relate here begins, and ends, with one such meeting. Or rather, it begins with a summons, one that would brook no argument.

★

I was expecting a parcel of books that Saturday morning, and when the knock came to the door in Cheyne Walk, I almost ran to answer, eagerly anticipating an afternoon of studious endeavor in my library among the pages of some new friends for my shelves. Instead I found a tall, heavily built lad on my doorstep.

At first glance I might have taken him for a policeman or a bruiser, for he had something of the manner of both, but his tone was polite, even cultured, as he handed me an envelope.

"I was told to pass this to you personally, sir," he said. "It is for your eyes only."

The envelope was plain, but of expensive paper and the handwritten note was done most elegantly in the blackest of black inks with not the slightest smudge on it. The wording of the note itself was equally as terse as the deliverer's message.

"I have sent my driver for you. Come immediately. It is of national importance."

I suspected the name even before I read it. It was appended, simply, 'Churchill'. I knew the man well enough from our previous encounters to know he would not be an easy chap to refuse.

I took enough time to fetch an overcoat, a hat, and my pipe and tobacco. The burly young chap stood, stock-still, filling my doorway the whole time, and only moved aside to let me exit. Then I was, if not exactly bundled, enthusiastically encouraged into a waiting carriage and within seconds we were off and away, heading east at some speed along the Embankment.

I had the interior of the rather well appointed carriage to myself, the bearer of the telegram having stepped up to sit with the driver. Once we passed Westminster, and didn't stop at Parliament, but continued to head even farther east, I realized it might be a longer trip than I had anticipated.

To pass the time, I read the note again, but it told me nothing new beyond the fact that Churchill was a man who expected to be obeyed. I hadn't heard from him since our last encounter, but I remembered reading of his appointment as First Lord of the Admiralty in *The Thunderer* a month or so back. I wondered if this summons might had something to do with that, but I had insufficient facts to hand for such conjecture, and settled for lighting a pipe, trying to enjoy the journey, and not letting my curiosity turn to frayed nerves and a bad temper.

The carriage kept going along the north side of the river, past St. Paul's and London Bridge, past the Tower, and headed into the warren of old quays and warehouses of the docks. I was starting to regret not having partaken of a larger breakfast.

I was still wondering quite how far I might have to travel when the carriage finally came to a halt at an old boat shed that, once upon a time, must have been one of the largest on the docks. There were a score or more of the young, strapping, silent type of chaps around. Some of them had made some kind of attempt at disguising themselves in old, frayed and worn clothing in an effort to pass themselves off as dockhands. But they weren't fooling me. This was Churchill's work all right, and these were his lads. I guessed they were military, or rather, given Churchill's post, Navy chaps to a man, and they were hard men, trained to kill by the look of them. I decided I had better be on my toes and keep my nose clean as I stepped down from the carriage onto the quay.

★

Churchill was there to meet me. He had grown more stout and portly since our last meeting, and his belly strained rather too tightly against his waistcoat. Compared to his lads around us, he looked out of place on the dock, his walking cane, heavy silver fob chain, tall hat and tails being much too grand, and more suited to the rarified atmosphere of the House.

Given the abrupt nature of my summoning, I half-expected him to be brusque and off-hand. But he was all 'hale fellow, well met' and made a show of telling his lads that I was an expert, consultant I believe is the word he used, and that I was to be given access to the whole site; nothing was to be kept from me. I still had no idea what was kept in the big shed at this point, but at least I knew now that I had been bought for a reason, for Churchill took my arm and suddenly became quite conspiratorial.

★

"It's those bally Huns. They're at it again," he said as he

led me toward the large boat shed and to a small door to the rear of the main building. "They're readying for war, I can feel it in my water. And it's my job now to do what I can to stop them mastering the seas. It's our best defense, always has been. But it's also our weakest point, for there are far too many miles of coastline all the way up the North Sea that are undefended and vulnerable to a sneak attack. We must show that we are prepared for any eventuality. Britannia must rule the waves again, and we must take charge of the oceans now, before it's too late. Don't you agree?"

It had sounded more in the nature of a speech than conversation, so I thought it best to be circumspect and muttered my agreement, to which he clapped me on the shoulder. It appeared we were to be friends, for a while at least.

We came to a halt outside the small door and he turned to me again.

"Now, Carnacki, my good man, I must ask for your complete discretion on this matter. What you are about to see is the best kept secret in the country at the moment, and we must ensure it remains that way. Apart from my chaps on guard here, there's only ten people know of it. And you are the tenth. The PM knows, but not the cabinet, and not even the King has been told. I know you are a man of your word, so I can trust you to keep this under your hat."

I nodded in reply, but didn't get time to get a word in edgeways as he continued.

"And there are to be no Friday night stories told around the fire over a smoke and a brandy; not with this one. It's too bally sensitive to be bandied about, even between close friends and confidantes. Agreed?"

"Agreed," I replied, although I was feeling increasingly unsure as to what I was letting myself in for. Churchill nodded to the guard beside the door, who opened it to allow us into the cathedral that was the boat shed and reveal Churchill's big secret.

Of all the things I had considered, of all the things I had expected to see, I think a German U-Boat might well have been near the bottom of the list.

★

And yet there it was, like a great russet-colored whale beached up on timbers that held it off the floor and ran along its whole length. The bulk of it almost filled the old shed from the huge riverside doors to the rear where we stood. I could only look at it in awe, and wonder how it had got here, to the East London docks. Churchill answered my question before I asked it.

"We think she's a prototype for a new class they're developing over there; there's been rumors of such a thing for a year or so now, and it looks like they were right. We caught this one snooping around in the North Sea, up in Doggerland at the shallowest point. Well, we didn't actually catch her. The engineers who've been over her bow to stern tell me that she had some kind of system failure and gave up the ghost all on her own. She was floating on the surface when we got to her, and not a man of the crew left alive inside either. The poor blighters all died of suffocation, or so the doctors assure me."

He paused, and laughed as if he had made a joke.

"Gave up the ghost. That's rather apt, I must remember that one."

"He didn't look inclined to explain that point, so I let it lie and went on to the matter that most concerned me.

"So you have a German submarine. That's probably good for you and the Admiralty," I replied. "But I fail to see why you need my particular brand of expertise, or where I am being asked to apply it."

Churchill laughed again, a booming thing that echoed high in the rafters of the shed.

"That is why you would never make a politician or indeed an Admiral, Carnacki. You have failed to see our tactical advantage here, even when it's right in front of your nose."

"I'm still not with you," I replied.

Churchill waved at the length of the submarine in reply.

"It felt like a godsend, when it turned up like that, almost on our doorstep," he said. "A free, no strings attached, chance to examine our largest adversary's latest vessel. But when I looked at it, I started to wonder. It was a simple question at first, but the implications of it kept making me come back to it again and again.

"What if we gave them it back? What if we gave them it back with something on board that would make them think twice about ever sending something our way again?"

I was starting to see some daylight, and I was wishing that I didn't.

"You want me to mock up some kind of propaganda scene inside the submarine, is that what this is about? I am to make it look like something from beyond killed the crew and that it has been taken over by a spectral presence? Parlor tricks and scare tactics, in other words."

"You've nearly got it, old man," Churchill said, and suddenly he looked completely serious. "But I do not, under any circumstances, want a mere mock up. There must be no 'parlor tricks' that can be easily exposed as such. I need the real thing. I want this U-boat infested with a particularly vicious spook, I went it sent back to them, and I want to put the fear of God into the bally Hun so that they will never trouble us again."

★

It took a few seconds for all of that to sink in. I did not know whether to be simply confused, or completely appalled. In the end, I pleaded unfit for the task at hand.

"You've seen my methods first-hand, Churchill," I said. "You know my defenses are just that; they are only defensive. I wouldn't know to go about calling up a spook, never mind ensuring you got a nasty, vicious one."

He didn't reply at first; he looked me straight in the eye for the longest time before speaking in a measured voice.

"Come, now. That is not strictly true, is it, Carnacki?" he said finally. "I know for a fact you have a wide variety of books on the shelves in your library dealing with such matters. There must be something in those tomes that is of practical use?"

I did not go into how he might know what I had in my private library. Just as he had seen my methods first-hand, so I had seen his. He had a ruthless streak in him I found hard to like, and a blatant disregard for any piddling matters such as legality and morality if they did not suit his purposes. He did however, have the strongest sense of duty to King and Country of any chap I have ever met, and I could not help but be impressed with the zeal with which he approached the task. But that in itself was not enough to get a job done that I considered to be frankly, impossible. I tried to tell him so in words he might understand.

"Those are merely books," I said. "It is only research and history. Practically, there is little there of use. Necromancy and demon summoning are only primitive methods of trying to understand the mysteries of the Outer Realms, and I have never encountered a single report that suggests any such attempts were ever successful. Let it go, Churchill. There is no foolproof way of summoning a thing from the Great Beyond, never mind getting one to do your bidding"

"I am not asking for it to be foolproof," Churchill said. "I am only asking for it to be done. Your country needs you, man. Will you refuse it in its hour of need?"

He did not know me well enough to realize that appeals to base patriotism wouldn't wash with me. My country was of little consequence compared to the immensity of the Beyond. But, still, it is my country and Mr. Churchill is a most persuasive gentleman.

I also had a feeling that if I did refuse him, I might not be making a return journey home from this boat shed. I have seen the shark beneath his smile, and his ruthlessness would not allow his secret to be out and abroad and not under his control. I would have to brazen it out with a brass neck until I could get a clearer idea of how I would need to play it to satisfy his demands.

"What manner of spook do you require?" I asked calmly, as if I knew what I was about.

★

He laughed at that, and hid the shark away. He did not fool me though; I knew it still swam in the depths, waiting to surface when required.

"I knew you were a man of sense," he said. "Come, let's seal our deal over a drink and a smoke and we can discuss it further."

He led me to a small office that was more like a foreman's hut at the back of the shed beyond the submarine propellers. The space was crammed with carpentry tools, blueprints, cameras and ledgers. And I was not in the least bit surprised to see my box of defenses on the floor amid the clutter, and two tall piles of my books on the table in a space that had obviously been cleared for them. It appeared that Churchill didn't only know the contents of my library; he had the run of the whole bally house.

At least he hadn't needed to have his chaps rifle my liquor cabinet or smokes drawer. He had a tall travelling valise at his side, one of those expensive leather and brass jobs I've had an eye on for myself. He opened it to expose, not books or clothes, but a well-stocked range of liquor in tall decanters, some expensive crystal glasses, and a long wooden cigar box.

He winked at me as he saw my astonishment.

"Perks of the job, old boy," he replied. "One must travel in style, if one must travel at all."

He poured me some rather fine single malt I hadn't had before from Orkney, and passed me a Cuban cigar that was thicker than my thumb and twice as long, before clicking his glass against mine.

"To business," he said after swallowing most of his scotch in a single gulp. I merely sipped at mine. I had a feeling I had a lot of work ahead of me, a feeling that was amplified considerably as he outlined his requirements.

"It has to be strange enough to spook the Huns," he said, "yet not so bloody weird that it'll frighten my men. I'm going to have to have some crew aboard when we take this thing out of here. They'll be needed to get it back into waters where it can be found."

"And what about the original German crewmen? How will their absence be explained?"

"Absence?" Churchill said, and again I saw the ruthless shark under the mask. "Oh, they won't be absent. We have them on ice in a shed not a hundred yards from here. When we're ready we'll get them back on board and send them off with their boat."

I was less and less keen on this whole business by the second, but I was in too far now to back out.

"I will need to spend some time with my books," I said. "This is not something I can undertake lightly."

Churchill nodded. He poured another large measure of his scotch and topped up mine, although I had as yet scarcely touched it.

"I thought you might say that," he said. "Let me know if you need anything. The chaps outside are at our beck and call at all hours."

He went and sat in the chair across the table opposite me and was immediately lost in his thoughts, a fug of cigar smoke surrounding him like fake ectoplasm at a séance.

It was time for me to get to work.

★

I sipped at the scotch and smoked the cigar as I checked to see what Churchill had thought were the books I might require for the task at hand. Not for the first time, he surprised me with his perspicacity and breadth of knowledge. He had indeed thought of everything, from the Key of Solomon to De Vermis Mysteriis, from several medieval grimoires to my working copy of the Sigsand mss. Of course, as I have said, I considered the bulk of this material to be of historical curiosity value only. I had read them all before, but never with an eye to considering them as in any way practical.

I took the time it took me to smoke the cigar to clear my mind of my own preconceptions, and then set about looking for something I thought might have a chance of working, given my talent and expertise, and a large amount of good luck. I had a feeling that I was going to need it.

★

I ploughed through spell after spell, annoyed at myself for agreeing to a course that took me so far from my natural instincts to defend against the very things I was going to attempt to raise. Much of the kind of ritual spellbinding I was perusing is, of course, superstitious mumbo-jumbo; dead men's hands, blood from a pregnant mare, the skull of a dog killed at a crossroads; all stuff and nonsense. And besides, procuring any such items in time for Churchill's purposes was going to problematic, to say the least. I aimed for something that might be simple, but effective, which proved to be another problem; the old coves responsible for writing these things didn't really go in for doing anything the easy way.

But finally I settled on something I found in 'The Mysteries of the Worm', a binding spell for summoning a hellish entity that could cloud men's minds and make them go mad at the sight of it. It sounded like the kind of thing that Churchill might be after, and even if it didn't work, I had the passage right there in the book to point at, to show him that I'd at least tried.

I was, however, not quite stupid enough to walk directly into a dark place and start chanting a centuries old demon summoning ritual. I would need some protection. I got up to check that nothing in my box of defenses had been damaged in its journey here.

Churchill looked up as I opened the box.

"Another snifter?" he said, and raised his empty glass.

"No," I replied. 'But I shall definitely need one when I return. I think I've found what you asked for."

"And will it work?"

"We shall know one way or another in a couple of hours."

★

It was mid afternoon and already starting to get rather dim inside the big boat shed as I carried my box of defenses up the makeshift gangway that led to the flat, main deck of the submarine. My footsteps clanged on metal and echoed, hollow, like funereal bells, all around me. The chill I immediately felt in my spine did not bode well for my state of mind to deal with what was coming next.

I considered setting up on that open, flat surface, but Churchill would want this job done properly. I would have to descend into the bowels of the beast so to speak. That was easier said then done, for there were no obvious exterior hatches. To get inside I had to manhandle the bally box up the railed steps of the turret, and back down the other side once I got inside. As a result, I was dashed hot and bothered before I even started to investigate the interior of the vessel.

I had enough light coming in from above me to open my box and get out the small oil lantern I carry within it. I lit it up, and started to look for somewhere I could set up my circles.

It was immediately obvious that I was going to have some difficulty. Conditions were cramped inside the submarine, to say the least, and there appeared to be no single spot of floor large enough to contain my defenses. The air inside the vessel felt heavy and slightly warm; it stank, of burnt oil and stale breath. To my left was a tall and wide bank of meters and dials I could make no sense of whatsoever, and to my right long lines of piping and wiring stretched off in both directions down the dark corridors. There was no sound save any that I was making, and even the tiniest movement, the merest scrape of sole on deck, was amplified in whispering echoes that ran up and down the length of the boat.

My lamp did not penetrate far into the darkness, and I was suddenly all too aware of Churchill's tale of the thirty dead crewmen who had met their end, locked in this metal box under who knows how many feet of cold water. That made my mind up for me. I could possibly have spent more time searching for a better, wider, spot, but now that I was here, I wanted to get things done as quickly as possible and get back to the bottle of scotch and some living company.

As I have said, I was in a tight spot. So I improvised. I stood in the main control area, which was slightly toward the bow under the turret, and set up a pair of small circles in chalk that were as wide as I could make them in the space I had available. Then I transcribed the pentagram, noticing that there was now only just, by a matter of inches, enough space for me to stand with my feet together inside the defenses. That, obviously, meant that my valves for the pentacle were much closer together than I would have liked, with only the span of a hand separating them, but I managed to quickly get them aligned in the peaks and troughs of the pentagram, and switched on the battery pack.

The resultant hum echoed and thrummed through the whole bally vessel, and a wave of cold rushed through the corridors, a cold, damp, breeze as if a heavy fog had descended.

My heart thudded faster, and my knees went to jelly before I remembered that I had stood in worse bally spots than this, facing real danger, not imagined spooks. I berated myself for letting the dark and Churchill's story get to me.

I stepped into the defenses, lit a pipe, and composed myself.

It was time to begin.

*

I will not reproduce the spell that I used here. Even inadvertent reading of these old incantations is thought by practitioners to cause unforeseen and unwanted effects, so it is probably for the best not to tempt fate. Besides, I did not get the opportunity to finish even the first stanza of the chant.

A great wall of darkness rushed at me out of the aft corridor, and all of the valves of the pentacle flared at once, so bright I was forced to close my eyes against the sudden brilliance. I heard the valves whine, and felt again the wave of cold and damp wash over and around me. I tasted salt spray at my lips.

When I opened my eyes again, I thought the brightness had temporarily caused a problem with my sight, for although I stood inside the shining pentacle, and color washed over and around me, there was nothing but black velvet dark beyond the boundaries of my circles.

I felt the weight of the darkness press against the pentacle, as if something solid were testing itself against the defenses. Cold seeped up from the deck, gripping at my ankles and calves as if I stood in a deep puddle of freezing water, and my teeth started to chatter until I clamped them down on the stem of my pipe.

The valves pulsed and whined and the green one in particular was under a deal of strain. The darkness got darker, the cold got colder, and I felt something in my mind, a searching, questing thought, as if the dark was looking for a way inside. I knew I had to resist. I could not succumb, for if I did I would never leave this vessel alive.

I started to recite an old Gaelic protection prayer that had proved efficacious for me in the past, mumbling through my clenched teeth, focussing all my attention on the words.

The darkness continued to press, hard, against all of my defenses. I struggled for breath, felt coldness pour down my throat, salty again, like the sea, and the dark swelled and closed in even tighter.

I summoned up all the strength I had in me and continued the Gaelic right through to its end. I called out the last words.

Dhumna Ort!

The blue valve blazed at my last shout, and all at once the blackness washed away, so suddenly it might never have been there at all. I stood there as the pentacle valves dimmed to a normal level and blood started to pump faster in my veins, warming parts that had been in danger of being frozen.

I had no need to call up one of Churchill's favored spooks.

There appeared to be one on board already.

★

Now that the darkness had washed away, and I could no longer feel any presence, every part of me wanted to step out of the circles and head up and out into warmer air, and a place where there was a large glass of good scotch waiting for me. But I knew Churchill's mind. He would want to know more of the nature of this new thing I had found, and how it could be pressed to become an advantage in his favor. And to do that, I would have to face the thing again.

I stood still and lit a fresh pipe. The taste of tobacco did much to remind me that I wasn't lost down here in the dark, that I was here of my own free will. I was here to learn.

The gray fug of smoke wafted away through the corridors of the vessel. My valves lit up enough of the corridors in front and behind of me to show that there was no sign of the wall of darkness. I knew, of course, that the thing had not simply departed for it is my experience that once an entity of the Outer Darkness arrives on this plane, they settle, and they are slow to leave.

I was proved right minutes later when the darkness gathered again in the forward corridor. As if it was aware of my presence now, it crept much more slowly than before. And as it was aware of me, so too, I was aware of it. It was less menacing this time, now that I knew it was there.

As before, the blackness gathered around the edges of my defensive circles, testing the boundaries of the valves; first the yellow one then the green flared and dimmed, flared and dimmed. Once again cold seeped into my lower limbs and damp air washed against me.

I knew what was coming next. This time, when the darkness sent out its dark probe to my mind, I grabbed hold of it and followed it back to the source, a mental projection trick that let me glimpse, however briefly, some of the thing's innate nature and intent. Fragments of what passed for its thoughts came to me, like images in my mind.

It was old, old and cold, and lost. It had slept for aeons in a deep place in the sea, undisturbed by storm or ice, lying, slumbering in the weed and stone, having been imprisoned even before the sea washed over it for the first time. Men had caught it, men wearing animal furs and wielding stone axes, wooden shields, and long forgotten ways of dealing with visitors from the Outer Darkness.

And so, it had slept, and dreamed for the longest time. And then, after an age of cold, dank, dark an iron thing came swimming in the waters above, breaking ancient bonds that the German submariners never even knew existed, allowing the darkness to surge and flow and fill them up.

I felt those poor German lads die, as if I had been the dark thing in the dark, and sudden, unbidden tears filled my eyes, and guilt hit me, hard. That broke my concentration, and alerted the dark to my presence.

It pushed against me hard, the shock almost sending me reeling outside the circles. The green valve flared and I thought I saw, for an instant, an even darker mass of blackness in the shadows, an amorphous, shifting, thing, that spoke a word in a language that I did not know but guessed the intent. There was only one thing this darkness wanted.

Home.

★

I spoke the Gaelic words again, and as before the blackness faded away, retreating down the corridors to wherever it was hiding itself in the bowels. This time I did not delay. I stepped out of the circles, left the pentacle on the deck and made my way quickly up the turret ladder, out to the boat shed above, then, almost running, down the gangway and into the foreman's office, where I headed straight for the scotch.

Churchill was sipping at a glass of his own, and puffing on another cigar. He raised an eyebrow and smiled thinly.

"I gather from your rather startled demeanor that you have had some success?"

I downed a couple of fingers and waited until it hit my stomach and spread its heat before answering.

"I had some failure, and some of what you might regard as success. Although I am not convinced that success is the proper word for what I have experienced."

He sat me down, and joined me in another drink. He tried to ply me with another of his, frankly enormous, cigars but I preferred the pipe. I puffed hard at it as I spoke, and he listened to my tale, without even the slightest hint of incredulity. He went quiet and thought for a few seconds before he spoke softly.

"So this thing in the dark that you saw? You believe it is what killed the Hun crew?"

"I believe so," I replied. "In fact, I am sure of it."

"I would like to see it for myself," he said.

I protested long and hard at that, but his final answer was what persuaded me.

"I will not ask my men to do something I would not do myself," he said, and by Jove, I think he meant it.

★

I went back with him as far as the deck of the submarine, but he bade me stand outside.

"As you did yourself, I will face this thing alone, in the same way as the men will have to face it to perform the task I must set for them."

I warned him to step over the circles into the inside of the pentacle, and not to break the protection once he was inside, no matter what might happen. I also gave him the last two words of the Gaelic chant, as a last resort should they be needed.

"Wish me luck, old chap," he said as he turned away. "I have faced many battles, but I do believe this short walk might be among the hardest things I shall be called to do for my country."

I agreed with him on that, but he went anyway. He was still chewing down hard on that infernal cigar as he climbed up and over, into the turret and down into the bowels of the sub.

I stood there for long minutes, straining to hear, waiting for a cry for help and ready to go to his aid if needed. For the longest time there was no sound save my own breathing and the slight hiss of burning tobacco in my pipe. Then, as if from a great distance, I heard it, a voice raised in a shout, the old Gaelic phrase repeated twice. It sounded as if the second time contained more than a trace of fear.

Dhumna Ort! Dhumna Ort!

I had started climbing up the turret when I heard scrambling sounds above me, and had to retreat as Churchill descended out of the sub with some haste. He did not stop to acknowledge me, but marched, almost running, away along the deck and down the gangway. By the time I reached the foreman's office, he was already making impressive headway down the scotch, gulping it down unceremoniously straight from the neck of the decanter.

He only spoke when he came up for air. His cheeks were now ruddy, but he was pale around the lips, with dark shadows under his eyes, and his hands shook badly as he lit a fresh cigar.

"That dashed thing killed the Huns," he said, and this time it wasn't a question.

But if I thought his experience might mean a change in course for his plan of action and a softening of his resolve, I was to be proved wrong with his next sentence.

"Can you show someone how to make that pentacle of yours? We will need one for each of the men. I shudder to think what might have happened had I not been inside it."

★

I spent the night sitting in that cramped little room, drinking and smoking with Churchill. Every so often he would call for one or another of his men and bark an order at them. But mostly we talked, of inconsequential matters; he spoke with some elegance, and not a little sense of regret, of his time as a journalist, and I regaled him with some of the tales that my friend Dodgson has already detailed in his journals. At some point I slept, and when I woke, Churchill was gone and about his business for King and Country.

As for myself, I never set foot inside the sub again after I retrieved my box of defenses the next morning. I spent two more days at the boat shed instructing Churchill's men in the art of pentacle defense, and showed some Naval engineers the trick of the valves and wires needed for their construction.

★

I heard no more for a week, then out of the blue I received another summons to the dockyard late of a Sunday evening.

The river was as quiet as it gets, and there was no ceremony. Firstly they loaded the dead Germans. I did not watch that part, for I was reminded all too vividly of the impressions I had received of their passing from the thing in the cold wet dark. I stood in the shed doorway smoking a pipe until that part of the job was done.

Then fifteen of Churchill's men went on board, each carrying a small bag of luggage and a box that closely resembled my own box of defenses. Churchill had a word and a handshake for every one of them, but if he had any qualms about what he was doing, they did not show.

Churchill and I retired to the hut at the rear again, where we shared more of his fine scotch until, almost an hour later the big shed doors were opened, the timber wedges were knocked away and the sub slid, almost silently into the river.

We went out onto the dock to watch it head off out toward the Estuary, a great dark shark cruising on the still waters.

"I don't know about the Germans," I said, "but it

certainly scares me."

"They will take her out into the North Sea and leave her floating as near to where we found her as they can manage," Churchill said. "Hopefully the Huns will find her before the sea claims her again."

"And your men? How will they return?"

Churchill looked at me, and now, for the first time, I saw how deeply he had been affected. He had fresh tears in his eyes.

"They have their orders," he said, turned his back on me and walked away.

I never heard of the fate of the submarine, or Churchill's men, and although I have met Churchill twice since, he has never spoken of it.

But some nights, when the fog rolls in from the river and I smell salt in the air, I dream of them cruising along in the deep dark, all dead at their posts while the cold blackness swirls around them.

I hope it was worth it.

The Edinburgh Townhouse

Carnacki's card of invitation that Friday morning had asked that we join him for supper a full hour earlier than was usual which indicated to me that he had a new story to be told, and one that might take some time. So it was with some degree of anticipation that I made my way to Cheyne Walk in Chelsea with only a short pause after work to change into my evening clothes. It was a most pleasant evening. On another occasion I might have tarried to watch the play of light on the river as the old city prepared for the weekend, but the thought of a long tale and good company meant that I strode quickly, all the way to Carnacki's doorstep.

The other chaps were already there ahead of me and we went straight to table, where the fare was, not for the first time, particularly Scottish in nature. There were cold medallions of venison and pickles to start with, and, to follow, a fine slab of fresh salmon with summer greens and potatoes, all washed down with a dark, heady, malted beer. I was quite full by the time our host led us through to the parlor, He gave us enough time to get our drinks charged and smokes lit before starting the tale of his latest adventure.

★

"I asked you here early this evening as this tale might take a while in the telling," Carnacki began. "And I would like to get it all done in one sitting, as it is rather a complex matter and I might have to explain too much of it all over again should we have to split it over two nights. Besides, I did not think you chaps would mind an extra hour with the contents of my liquor cabinet.

"As you have probably surmised from our supper, I was

taken to Scotland again a journey which, for me at least, never feels like a hardship despite the long miles between there and here.

"It all began simply enough, ten days ago, when I received a morning letter from a police sergeant in Edinburgh. He begged my indulgence, citing the name of a mutual friend, a retired Army General I had helped some months back, as evidence of his sincerity, and asked for my aid in a matter that had him, and most of the local constabulary, completely stumped. Mention was made of a haunting, and not only one at that, but a variety of different spooks and specters. I didn't put too much credence in that; we all know that the Scots can be a superstitious lot as a whole. And the sergeant was indeed rather vague on particulars. But his note had just the right amount of intrigue and hints of a supernatural agency at work that I could do little but reply by telegram, stating that I would see him as soon as possible and that he should expect me on the afternoon train.

"An hour later I was at Kings Cross Railway Station and heading for points north accompanied by my luggage and the smaller of my two boxes of protections. The journey was uneventful, the lunch on board just this side of edible, and we made good time such that I arrived in Edinburgh in the late afternoon feeling none the worse for wear for the traveling.

"My sergeant was on the platform to meet me. He was a stout, well-fed chap in his forties, balding on top, with bristling ginger whiskers, a bulbous nose that told of a fondness for a drop of liquor, and a most kindly face. He introduced himself in a soft local Edinburgh accent as Andrew Carruthers.

"'Damned happy to see you, Mr. Carnacki. The General won't hear a bad word said about you; he says you're the man to rid us of this bogle.'

"He tagged along at my side as I booked myself into the North British for two nights, then, as the clock was ticking around to five-thirty, we made our way by carriage down to the Grassmarket. I took my box of protections with me. On the way, the sergeant gave me more detail as to why he had asked for my help.

"'The old house has always had a bad reputation, Mr. Carnacki,' he said. 'Even when I was a lad we used to dare each other to creep up and peer in through the thick warped windows at the side. And I'm not afraid to say that on a couple of occasions, we thought we saw something, something squat and dark, shifting in the corners of the empty rooms.'

"'So the house is derelict? It is lying empty?' I asked.

"The sergeant shook his head.

"'That's the problem, Mr. Carnacki. What with the gentrification of the area in recent years, the older properties as have been empty for a while have been renovated and sold on. I hear there's good money to be had for those that have the energy for it. This particular old house has been turned into several smaller apartments. It's all a tad too cozy for my liking, and not unlike a warren of rabbits all living on top of each other. But that seems to be what the younger generation is after. The developer has been working on this one since the turn of the year and it's nearly ready to be sold.'

"'So what, precisely, is the problem?'

"'Well, sir, it's hard to tell, precisely. There's things moved around when nobody's around, weird shuffling noises in the stairwells, that kind of thing. But the other officers who've been called out to the disturbances won't go back. They're staying well clear, and, as I think I have already mentioned, there's talk of a bogle.'

"'I've heard talk of Scottish bogles before,' I replied. 'And most are simply a fear of old dark places.'

"'All the same, sir, there's something far wrong with that house. You'll see for yourself soon enough. You can feel it as soon as you walk in the door.'"

★

"The property was one of those tall, old, hefty affairs sitting off the road in the shadow of the castle rock and it looked rather dilapidated from the outside, having fallen from any stately glory it once had some centuries past. It was obvious that attempts were being made in its restoration. New iron railings lined the short line of steps up to the doorstep and the front windows were set in new, and newly painted, wooden frames. The front door itself was solid enough and had been painted a rather garish, to my eyes, shade of red that matched the pillar-box in the road outside.

"And you know what? The chap was right about the bally place not feeling right. As soon as he opened the door and we stepped inside I felt it. It was not exactly a presence but more a certain quality to the air, a strange timbre in the echoes of our footsteps in the empty hallway.

"It was a feeling I knew only too well, but there was something else here too; I had the distinct impression that I too had been recognized, and been given a welcome.

"'The developer chap has had a lot of trouble with the workmen,' the sergeant said. I saw that he was hanging back in the doorway, not wishing to take too many steps away from a quick escape should it be warranted. 'There's been three different crews over a six month period that I know of, and all of them have cried off the job for one reason or another.'

"I stood still for several moments, taking my time in gauging the feel of the place. I already knew there was a presence here that merited further investigation, but I would need more time, and information, before I could mount a proper inquiry. I tried to get what morsels I could from the constable.

"'These disturbances you mentioned, are they centered anywhere in particular?'

"'Things tend to happen in the stairwell, sir, or so I've heard; there and in the cellar, basement, whatever you call it. Down there's the room we used to peer into from the window round the side. That is where they say the bogle lives.'

"I wondered, not for the first time, whether the semi-mythical 'they' had any names, or whether it was all merely hearsay. I didn't get a chance to ask as the poor chap had suddenly gone quite pale and looked like he might even pass out on me.

"He only revived when I got him back out into the street, where we had a smoke while contemplating the old castle walls high above us. He still wasn't quite recovered, so we went along the road twenty yards or so to a bar where a pint of strong ale and a meat pie did much to bring him to his former self.

"'I am very sorry, sir,' he said. 'I don't know what came over me. It's that house. It has always made me feel proper queer.'

"I assured him that it was a normal reaction for me to see in my line of work, and we chatted as we finished our beer. I did not learn anything more about the house though, and I was loath to broach the subject unless it brought on another funny turn in the poor officer. I could only ponder as to what manner of thing would have such an effect on what appeared to be a well-balanced and strong minded, individual.

"When we left the bar, the sergeant started walking away, heading for Cowgate to take him back to the town, center. He stopped when he noticed I did not follow.

"'I'm heading back across the road,' I said. 'To see what's what.'

"'Surely you do not intend to spend the night in there alone, Mr. Carnacki? Alone in the dark?'

"I could see that the thought of it discomfited him rather unduly.

"'I do indeed,' I replied. 'Or at least the early part of it, until I discover the cause of your 'bogle'. I have left my box of defenses there for that purpose.'

"I saw the look that passed across his face, fear and duty fighting for supremacy. I had been right in my assessment of the chap, for despite an obvious funk, his duty proved to be the stronger.

"'Then I shall stand with you,' he said, although he did not look to be the slightest bit happy at the prospect.

"I patted him on the shoulder.

"'There's really no need to bother yourself, old man, and besides, I work best when I'm left on my own to potter about. Come and see me in the North British in the morning and I shall tell you the story of what has happened over breakfast.'

"He looked like a man who was not sure that I would be still alive by breakfast, but I could also see his relief that his duty did not call for him to join me. We parted in the road, and I made my way over to the townhouse, arriving on the doorstep as the last rays of the day's sun were being cast over the old castle high above."

★

"I had to work quickly to set up a defensive circle as the light was fading fast and there did not appear to be even so much as a gas fitting in the building, despite it's obvious recent renovations.

"I decided to set up for the duration in the hallway as that way I had a view both of the stairs and of the door that led down to the cellar. I also decided not to deploy the electric pentacle until I had a better idea of what might be going on in the house. If I was being watched, as I suspected to be the case, I did not want to play my best cards too early in the hand.

"Using a plumb and chalk, I quickly set out the inner and outer circles and made my usual lines on the floor inside them, going over the chalk with garlic and salt. I lit the small oil lantern I had in the box and sat on the box itself in the middle of the circles as the light finally left the sky and darkness fell in the hallway.

"I sat, puffing on my pipe and watching the play of smoke and light from where the light from the tall lamppost outside came in through the half-moon window above the door. After a while the street outside grew quieter, the day's trade done, and there was only the occasional clatter of wheels on cobbles to remind me that I was not all alone in existence.

"I cannot really describe the feeling in the old house as both it and I settled down to wait for what the night might bring. The air felt heavy and oppressive, and there was a palpable air of tension, as if something was holding its breath, waiting for me to make a move."

★

"As I have said, I was sitting on my wooden box, facing the door, but as I had earlier, I began to feel a sense that I was being watched. This time it felt as if there was something at my back, at the top of the stairs on the first landing, something that was even now gazing at me down the stairwell.

"The feeling became so intense, so certain that I almost took a bally blue funk and got out of there right then. But as you know, I have stood in the dark in the face of many perils, and those experiences stood me in good stead at that moment. Besides, I would never be able to face the sergeant at breakfast if my tale was only that I had fled with my tail between my legs at the first sign of his 'bogle'. It would only serve to confirm his suspicion and cement the legend that was growing around the house. No. I had been asked to give of my expertise, and I owed the man my best shot at it.

"I steeled myself for what I might see, and turned around and sat facing the stairway. And immediately the sense of being watched grew stronger still. I don't know how I knew, but I was sure there was something there at the top of the flight of stairs, sitting in the dark, hunched on the landing, watching me.

"The darkness up there gathered and swirled, and a smell assaulted my nasal passages. It was thick, cloying, animalistic and strangely, disconcertingly familiar. Something sniffed and snuffled, the darkness moved again, and I caught a glimpse of the watcher, one that made me stand so suddenly I almost knocked the box across the pentacle.

"What I saw was something from one of my own nightmares, a face part man, part porcine. Pink eyes stared at me, unblinking. A stubby snout raised in the air and snuffled loudly. I saw vapor breathe from at the flaring nostrils before, like smoke in wind, the swine thing turned away and vanished into the dark shadows above me."

★

Carnacki's tale was interrupted by an interjection from Arkwright.

"Not those bally swine things again, Carnacki. Please, not them. I had blasted nightmares for weeks after your last encounter."

Carnacki smiled sadly.

"I am afraid so, old friend. And the tales are, unfortunately, intricately linked, so I cannot tell this one without some mention of the other, and the beasts, as you will see, are relevant, as much in this case as they were in the other. But fear not, this is not their tale, at least not entirely so, although they do play their part. They are merely a manifestation and a small part of a bigger picture.

"But let us not get ahead of ourselves. Let me return

you to that night, and the defensive circles in the dark townhouse hallway. This tale needs to be told in the proper order for it to be told properly."

*

"As it turned out, I had seen all I was going to be allowed to see for that first night," Carnacki began again. "The feeling of oppressive weight in the hallway lifted, the air suddenly smelled fresher and clearer, and I no longer had the feeling of being watched.

"I had been given a message though, my presence had been noted, and the nature of my adversary had been revealed. It was now up to me to decide what to do with this information.

"I sat there in the dark for a good twenty minutes, waiting to see whether there would be any further manifestations. I saw only dark and shadow, and heard nothing more than the normal settling and creaks one encounters in old properties once the sun has stopped heating them for the day.

"I left my defensive circles and stepped out onto the boards of the hallway. Although I took care to remain within stepping distance of the chalk lines, nothing attempted to attack me. If I had so wished, I believe I could have had the run of the whole bally building right then, but I was in no mood then to undertake an exploration of the rest of the house. That was certainly not anything I wanted to attempt in the dark, even with a lantern at hand.

"I retrieved the lamp from the circles, snuffed it out before putting it back, and headed for the door. I was already looking forward to a spot of late supper and a soft bed in the North British. But the house wasn't quite as done with me as I had imagined."

"As I reached the main doorway and put a hand on the lock, I heard a snuffling again, not from the stairwell, but from behind the door to the cellar, as if it was taunting me to investigate.

"I remembered well my previous encounters with the beasts, and how powerful these swine things could be. To attempt any action without having the electric pentacle deployed would be an act of folly on my part. Besides, I had by this time decided on my course of action for the night.

"I went out into the Grassmarket, closed the door firmly behind me, and hailed a carriage to take me back to my hotel where I did indeed have a most pleasant late supper before retiring to bed."

★

"I slept soundly, rising at seven for my ablutions and a brisk walk in the gardens below Princes Street. On my return to the hotel, I met the sergeant in the downstairs dining room for breakfast and told him what had occurred over an excellent plateful of black pudding, bacon, eggs and toast.

"'You saw the bogle?' he said in hushed tones, as if astonished that I was still alive, and as amazed that I was able to both eat and talk rationally and had not been completely paralyzed with fear.

"'I not only saw it, I recognized it,' I replied, and this time it was the sergeant who was unable to form a coherent sentence.

"And then there was nothing for it but to put him out of his misery and relate for him my previous encounter with the porcine beasts. Over several mugs of strong coffee and a few pipes of tobacco, I told my tale of the Dark Island, and the house that sat on the borderlands of time and space.

"I kept his Lordship's name out of it of course, and did not specifically mention the location, but I gave him the basics. I told the sergeant, as I have told you chaps before, my theory of how the swine things were protectors of the veil between this world and the majesty of the wider wonders beyond. I related how I believed them to be a buttress against the insanity that waited if we were to look at it all at once, and how they are often to be encountered in such places as where the veil is thin between here and the Outer Darkness.

"I could see that the poor chap was struggling to comprehend the enormity of what I was telling him. I stopped before I got to the part about the great black pyramid and the vastness of the dark places in the far future beyond; I have enough trouble comprehending that particular enormity for myself without inflicting it on someone encountering the idea for the first time.

"'It is not a bogle then?' he asked once I was done.

"'Well, there are bogles, and there are bogles. But as I say, I have met its kind before, and lived to tell the tale, so if it is a bogle, it is not one we need too greatly fear.'

"'And can it be got rid off? Can you clean the house of it?'

"That was a question I had hoped he would not ask, for it was one for which I did not, as yet, have an adequate answer.

"I fended the question by telling him my plan of action, and giving him something to do. Remembering how efficacious one had proved to be in the previous case, I sent the sergeant off in search of an iron bar or poker, and after another smoke and a pot of strong tea it was time to return to the townhouse.

"I left the hotel, decided it was too fine a day to waste on a carriage journey, and took a most pleasant walk up through the valley of closes adjoining the High Street, across the castle esplanade, and down the West Bow to the Grassmarket."

★

"I was intending to spend some time in setting up my electric pentacle, and then in investigating the other rooms of the house before nightfall. However, I was delayed in my task even before I could get started, when I met a young, pale looking, chap standing on the doorstep of the house.

"He looked somewhat lost, and slightly embarrassed as I went up the short flight of steps to meet him in the doorway. When he spoke, it was with a French accent, although his English was as good as yours or mine, and better than Arkwright's will ever be. He was clean-shaven and bright eyed, with a mop of that particular kind of dark, lustrous hair that only those born near the Mediterranean seem to be blessed with. His woolen, worsted suit was of the best quality and his boots looked to be of the finest leather, so I immediately took him as coming from money.

"'Excuse me, sir,' he asked. 'I must ask you. Are you the

current owner of this property? I understand it is for sale, and I should very much like to purchase it.'

"Of course, I had to explain to him that I was not in a position to help him at that moment. That involved me explaining, in part, the reason for my being there at the door, and I was not quite able to disguise the rather unusual, to the public eye, nature of my business.

"My explanation did not seem to worry him in the slightest. Indeed, I think he had expected something of that nature.

"'But you do know how to contact the owner?' he asked, and went on when I nodded. 'In that case, I have a story, and a proposition, that I would like you to pass on in my behalf, if you will allow me to tell it?'

"And so it was that a mere ten minutes later, and rather earlier in the day than I am used to, I found myself back in the bar I had visited with the sergeant. I sipped at more of the fine strong Edinburgh ale, while hearing another story, this time from my new young French friend."

★

"I shall not tell you his whole story, for it is a long, and unfortunately rather sad one, and one that is most personal to him. Suffice to say he was but recently bereaved from his young wife of a mere two years and the poor chap had been quite lost in grief for the greater part of the time since her passing some four months previous to our meeting on the doorstep.

"That grief had, in turn, led him down dark pathways, and it finally taken him to a house in Paris where he had been promised that he might meet his lady again. As he spoke, I was able to take a guess at where his story was leading.

"I don't have to tell you chaps my opinion of those that prey on the recently bereaved, as you have heard it all before. The parlor spiritualist con artist is one of the biggest barriers to progress in my line of research, for they do much to muddy the waters in the minds of the general public, and serve only to discredit the work of far better, and less corrupt, minds than theirs.

"But our young man; by now I had discovered his name

to be Bernard Thibaut, told me, with great sincerity, that his quest had met with some success in Paris, and that his presence here in Edinburgh was the next stage of his journey. He had been told that there was a special place waiting for him, and I shall relate to you, as he told it to me, what he says was told to him in Paris.

"'I believe that the old house is one of a few special houses that are spread all over the world. Most people only know of them from whispered stories over campfires; tall tales told to scare the unwary. But some, especially those of us who suffer, know better. The bereaved and the lost are drawn to these places to ease their pain. There, if you have the will, if you have the fortitude, you can peer into another life, where loved ones are not gone, where loved ones wait for us, and where we both might live together forever.'

"Poppycock, or so I thought, but the poor chap was completely obsessed with the idea, and now that he was sitting a matter of yards from his goal, he was not to be dissuaded. I made my own thoughts on the matter quite clear to him.

"I scoffed at the very idea of a bally haunted house that was some kind of coaching inn for trysts with the dearly departed. As you know, I do not believe such things are possible, but he was most sincere, and would not be swayed.

"'I saw it for myself in Paris. I can only ask that you believe my sincerity in the matter. Being a rational man, you will want to know how it works, Mr. Carnacki. I cannot tell you that. I was told that no one has ever known, only that the houses are the important part, and that a sigil and a totem are needed as the price of entry.'

"'Sigil?' I asked, and young Bernard rolled up his right sleeve. He had a green stemmed, white flowered, lily tattooed on his inner forearm, a precisely detailed, most delicate thing that trembled as he pulled his sleeve back down to hide it.

"'A marking of the flesh with something that was important to both you and your beloved, that is the nature of the sigil. And my totem comes from my lady herself.' He drew out a small gold locket from where it was on a chain under his shirt and showed me the curled lock of dark hair inside it. 'With the sigil and the totem in my possession, and with me in the special place where the veil is thin, my lady can come, and we can be together again.'

"I believe I might have started at his mention of the veil, so much so that I almost spilled some of my ale. I had been dismissing his story entirely. But his mention of the curtain between worlds, along with my sight of the swine thing the night before, and my knowledge of how the veil could appear to bend time itself, combined to have me thinking that perhaps his tale might not be so outlandish after all.

"Of course, after hearing his story, it was only polite of me to recount my own. Bernard got rather excited as I explained my area of expertise, the reason for my being in Edinburgh, what I suspected of the veil, and how I intended to stand vigil in the hallway for another night.

"'It is no mere happenstance that we have met here, Mr. Carnacki,' he said. 'The house has brought us together for a reason.'

"He insisted that he would join me in my attempt to delve into the house's secrets, and there was something so infinitely sad and forlorn about the poor chap that I did not have the heart to say no to him. Besides, he was proving do be good, if somewhat melancholy, company and proved a fine conversationalist once I got him nudged off the topic of death and the afterlife.

"We had another pint of beer and a spot of early lunch in the bar before heading over to the house to start our preparations for the evening. On arriving at the townhouse, I found an iron bar on the doorstep. The good Sergeant had done the task I had set for him, but he had not had the strength of will to even open the door to leave the cold iron in the hallway."

★

"Bernard did not seem perturbed to see my chalk markings on the floor and asked some astute questions as to the nature of the electric pentacle as I set out my valves and wires and small battery. I smoked one of his overly perfumed cigarettes as I told him of my color theory, and how it has been tested in a variety of cases and situations, and he followed my train of thought easily enough despite the language differences.

"But I could tell he also had other things on his mind. His gaze kept turning to the closed doors to the other apartments, and to the one on the left-hand side nearest the entrance in particular.

"He stepped over in that direction, and even put a hand on the door, but was halted by a sudden sound from beyond the door on the opposite side of the hallway.

"A snuffling, sniffing noise that I recognized only too well came from behind the cellar door."

★

Arkwright interjected into Carnacki's story again,

"I knew it. I knew those blasted piggy blighters would be back. Give them what for, Carnacki."

Of course, as soon as he realized he had broken the flow of the story, the poor chap was quite apologetic. Carnacki waved away his pleas for forgiveness away with a smile.

"I was going to stop around this point anyway and ask if anyone needed to recharge their glasses or get a smoke lit. We have a way to travel yet tonight together, gentlemen, and fresh worlds, if not exactly to conquer, at least to investigate.

"So come, let us try some of the new bottle of scotch I brought back with me from my sojourn. It is an Islay malt with which I am unfamiliar and I am keen to have a taste."

The scotch did indeed prove to be most excellent, and we all partook of Carnacki's generosity in its pouring, then lit up fresh smokes and prepared for the next part of his tale.

He kept us in suspense for a minute while refilling his old pipe and getting it lit, then continued.

★

"The beast on the other side of the door fell quiet.

"Bernard and I held our breath, waiting to see if there would be a recurrence of the sound, but none came. We were still only in the early afternoon and hours away from darkness so I did not want to switch on the pentacle, for fear my battery would not last through what might be required of it in the night. I was, therefore, quite relieved when it appeared that silence and calm was once again going to be restored.

"Bernard headed for the door on the left hand side again. This time there was no snuffling from the cellar, so he put out a hand and turned the handle. I was by his side as he pushed the door open. I expected to be looking into an empty room, but that was not the case at all.

"There were people inside, but it was as if a glass wall was stretched over the doorway. We could not step forward, we only stand and watch, spectators watching a scene as if it were playing on a stage in front of us. And this was no magic lantern show, no flickering, jerky movement. This was as real as we are here and now. We saw it all in minute, sharp, detail. And although we could not pass through the plane of the doorway, we could hear the conversation from inside well enough.

"We looked inside to see a small woman standing over a bulky man, who sat in a kitchen chair. They were both drinking. It was scotch, I could smell it, and they were smoking strong cigarettes, which I could also smell. There was the faintest hint of aniseed or liquorice wafting through to me, French, like the one I had been smoking earlier.

"The woman looked to be barely five feet tall, the paleness of her face accentuated by jet-black hair that hung in a single long plait to tickle her waist. Her clothes were equally black, a floor-length dress giving her the appearance of a hole in the fabric of reality. She glided rather than walked.

"'I am the concierge,' I heard her say, 'but you already know that. What you do not know is what that title means, here in this place.'

"'I live here, in number one,' she said. 'But you could have number three if you like? Number six is empty, but you wouldn't like that. The last concierge had that one, and he wasn't as fastidious in his habits as some; it might be years before it's ready for somebody else.'

"While she was speaking, I was trying to take in all the details of the scene, trying to fix it in my memory so that I could record it later.

"Her apartment looked to have been transported wholesale from a continental townhouse of some antiquity; it was decorated with heavy wood furniture, mostly mahogany by the looks of it, and polished to within an inch of its life. There was dark red flock wallpaper, portraits of the long dead which were presumably family, and a thick crimson pile carpet that had seen its best days many decades before. A gas fitting in the wall provided the only source of light, sending flickering shadows dancing everywhere. Directly opposite the doorway there was a long wall covered totally in bookshelves housing leather-bound volumes that looked older still than the furniture. Dark velvet curtains, deep red, almost purple, were pulled shut, covering the windows that overlooked the street.

"I was wondering at that moment which street I would be looking out over should I be able to enter and draw back the curtains; I suspected it would not be in Edinburgh."

★

"While I had been looking around, the conversation between the room's occupants was still ongoing.

"'You will have questions?' the concierge said to the man.

"'I will have questions,' he agreed. 'I will have many of them. Here is an easy one to start with. What in blazes is going on here? Something brought me here, I know that much. I felt its tug and pull in my head and in my gut. But what is it? Is it some kind of hypnotism or even some kind of drug?'

"The woman replied with almost the same bally spiel that Bernard had given me in the bar bot n hour before.

"'There are houses like this all over the world. Most people only know of them from whispered stories over campfires; tall tales told to scare the unwary," she went on. "But some of us, those who suffer...some of us know better. We are drawn to the places, the loci if you like, where what ails us can be eased. Yes, dead is dead, as it was and always will be. But there are other worlds than these, other possibilities. And if we have the will, the fortitude, and a sigil, we can peer into another life, where the dead are not gone, where we can see that they thrive and go on. And as we watch, we can, sometimes, gain enough peace for ourselves that we too can thrive, and go on.

"'You will want to know more than why. You will

want to know how. I cannot tell you that. None of us has ever known, only that the place is important, and a sigil and totem are needed. Those are the constants here.'

"She puffed contentedly again for several seconds. Smoke went in, but very little, if any, came back out, soaked away and down inside her.

"I wondered whether she might be full of the stuff, whether there might indeed be nothing inside her but swirling smoke.

"I had to pay attention, for the concierge was speaking again.

"'If you still want to stay after what you have seen here today, you must agree to my terms,' she said. It wasn't a question, and the man nodded in reply.

"'How can I not stay? All I ever wanted is here, somewhere in this house. I need to be here, with her. It's all I'll ever need.'

"'Then it's decided. You'll take number three. Once we get you settled and your things moved in, there will be more rules, all of which are for your own safety while you are here. But first things first. You will need a sigil, for that is your connection to the Great Beyond, and it is the way that the Veil knows to allow you access.'

"The man motioned at his belly. There was plenty of it under his shirt.

"'You mean I'm to get cut? Here?'

"She smiled.

"'Wherever you want it. Cut, or tattooed, or even drawn on with pen and ink. It is the voluntary marking of the flesh that is the important thing. Don't ask why. I can't tell you. All I know is what I was told myself. Just putting it on paper doesn't work. In fact, it could open ways that the veil does not control, and that way lies madness, then death soon after. So it must be the sigil, and it must be on flesh. The fact that it works is all I know. It has to be taken on faith.'

"'You do know what I do for a living?' the man said, rather too harshly. 'Faith is not normally a word in my vocabulary.'

"'Then learn it,' she said, raising her voice. 'That, or leave right now and don't come back. I don't really care either way. I'm not here to mother you, or be your confessor. I'm the concierge. If you want to talk, I'll listen if I feel like it. But my job is to look after the house and make sure you continue to have access to the veil. That takes up most of my time. The occupants need to be able to look after themselves.'

"'So at least tell me what this sigil has to look like?'

"She went back to laughing. It suited her better than a frown.

"'It can be anything you like, as long as it's yours,' she said, lighting a fresh smoke from the butt of the previous one. 'As long as it provides the required connection with that which you desire the most.'

"'I want to get cut. That'll ensure it's permanent .I want it to be permanent. Do I have to do it myself?'

"She laughed louder at that, and the glass in the light fixture tinkled in sympathy.

"'Oh no. That would be barbarous. Of course, you can if you want to, but think of the potential for you to make a mess of it? Others have taken a more artistic approach and, if I may say so, I have a way with a blade myself that would make the experience much more pleasant than other methods you might choose. Would you allow me?'

"She smiled again, but now she looked more like a predatory bird eyeing its prey.

"The man stubbed out his cigarette and drained the Scotch.

"'Let's have at it then. I'm ready.'

"'We'll see about that,' she replied. She sucked another prodigious draw from her own smoke and stubbed it out before lifting a knife from a counter.

"It was at that precise moment that the door of the room slammed shut with a bang that rang throughout the house. Silence fell around us once more. We looked at each other, neither of us able at that moment to articulate our thoughts as to what we had seen.

"When Bernard pushed the door open again, it was to reveal an empty room, with no furniture, no people, and no concierge."

★

"Once again Bernard looked at me. It was not fear I saw in his eyes. It was wonderment.

"'You saw too? You saw the lady? You heard the concierge?'

"I nodded.

"'I saw. But I have the feeling any message that was sent here was meant for you, rather than for me.'

"Bernard fell quiet for a time at that. We smoked, each lost in our thoughts. I chose my pipe this time, having had my fill of the smell of aniseed. It was the young Frenchman who broke the silence, with a question I had been considering myself.

"'I wonder if there are other scenes to be watched in the other rooms?'

"Of course, after that, there was nothing for it but to go and have a look."

★

"There was still plenty of light so I had little trepidation in approaching the stairs, especially when I looked up the well to see the dome of a glass skylight high overhead at the top of the building. Thin watery sunlight washed all across the upper landing.

"We decided to work from the uppermost level down. There were four floors, including the bottom one where we started, and the rooms were numbered, so that numbers seven and eight were on the top landing. I felt my blood pumping hard as I approached number eight, for the day had been rather weird and strange already, and it was still the afternoon.

"I was having far too much excitement for one day to my liking.

"But I need not have worried. The apartment beyond the door to number eight was empty and bare of any furniture whatsoever, a clean slate waiting for an occupant. Number seven proved equally empty, as did the two apartments on the next landing down. By the time we reached the door of number four, I was feeling confident that we were in for no further alarms on the way down.

"We had found another empty apartment in number four and turned away when a cloud moved across the sun, casting dark shadows in the corners of the landing where we stood. I smelled it again; heavy, animal, must, and so thick I could almost taste it.

"One of the shadows opposite us on the landing swirled and grew darker, and, from within it, something snuffled and sniffed at us."

"I decided that discretion was the better part of valor at that moment. I led Bernard downstairs toward the pentacle, ready to step into the defensive circles should it be required, but as we reached the foot of the stairs the cloud passed on and sunlight washed across the stairs again. When I looked up to the landing, there was nothing up there but dancing motes of dust."

★

"I knew that the door to room number two, the one I had heard snuffling behind the previous night, didn't lead to a room at all. It led down to the cellar, and all of a sudden I was thinking of porcine beasts and dark shadows again. The sunlight most certainly was not going to pierce that far down. I took precautions before opening the door and when I finally did so, Bernard was behind me holding the lit lantern, and I had the hefty iron bar in my hand, its weight doing much for my feeling of security.

"I opened the door slowly, half-expecting a snuffling swine thing to be there on the other side ready to pounce. But there was only quiet and dark.

"We went down slowly. The stairs were old. They had not been renovated to the same standard as those in the main body of the house, and aged timbers creaked underfoot. We went down ten wooden steps, then a bottom six of stone. We were now below street level and the air here was colder, almost frigid. My breath steamed ahead of me, and I wished I had been wearing a heavier jacket.

"The stone steps opened out onto a low-ceilinged basement that ran under the full extent of the old house. Most of the area was shored up with red brick, that was badly pointed and cracked in places, but the far wall from where we stood was rough-hewn stone, as if it had been hacked straight out of the bedrock. The whole area was cloaked in semidarkness, lit by dim sunlight coming in from two high windows up at the roof level. I wondered whether, perhaps, on another day, I might look up there and see a young, fresh faced, sergeant and his friends looking in.

"It appeared that the contents of the old, pre-renovation house had been piled, willy-nilly down here to rot. White sheets covered aged, battered furniture, stacks of books had been piled up in the corners, old paintings and portraits sat stacked against the walls, and dusty mirrors reflected my own pale, tense expression back at me at every turn.

"As you chaps know, I am used to quiet. Indeed, quiet is normal for an old building, but this felt deeper than that. It felt almost sepulchral, and to make any sudden noise down here would have felt like talking too loudly in a silent church. Nothing moved, and all I heard was the thudding of my heartbeat in my ears.

"A heavy carriage rumbled along the road outside and I felt the vibration through my soles before the silence descended completely again. But it had achieved a purpose. It had reminded me that beyond the high windows, a whole city was going about its business. We might be alone in this cold basement, but help was always going to be close by if it were to be required.

"I had started to relax a tad when something moved in the left-hand corner of the cellar. I was ready to head back for the stairs if there had been even the slightest hint of a snuffle or smell of a beast. But this proved to be something else entirely.

"It started small; a tear in the fabric of reality, no bigger than a sliver of fingernail, appeared and hung there. As I watched it settled into a new configuration, a black oily droplet held quivering in empty air.

"The walls of the cellar throbbed like a heartbeat. The black egg pulsed in time. And now it was more than obvious. It was growing.

"It calved, and calved again, and even as it did so I realized I knew what I was looking at. This too I had seen before, and this too was another manifestation of the Veil, the gateway to beyond. I had been right in my surmise. The veil was indeed thin here, even perhaps too thin, given the ease with which reality flowed and distorted.

"The room kept throbbing.

"Four eggs hung in a tight group, pulsing in time with the rising cacophony of the chanting. Colors danced and flowed across the sheer black surfaces; blues and greens and shimmering silvers on the eggs.

"In the blink of an eye there were eight.

"We had no thought of escape, lost in contemplation of the beauty before us.

"Sixteen now, all perfect, all dancing.

"The throbbing grew louder still.

"Thirty two now, and they had started to fill the cellar with dancing aurora of shimmering lights that pulsed and capered in time with the throb.

"Sixty-four, each a shimmering pearl of black light.

"The colors filled the room, crept around our feet, danced in my eyes, in my head, all though my body.

"A hundred and twenty eight eggs now, and already calving into two hundred and fifty-six.

"By Jove, it was seductive. I had the mysteries of the cosmos right there, close enough to reach out and touch. I cannot tell you chaps how much I wanted to step forward, be part of it and see where it might take me.

"I might even have gone, been lost to you forever, had young Bernard not gripped my arm, and directed my attention to a growing swirl of darkness to our right. Something stood, to one side of the growing mass of black eggs, watching us. I recognized it immediately.

"It was the same manner of beast I had encountered on the Dark Island, the same thing I had seen on the stairs the night before. Another swine thing had manifested itself. This one was most definitely male. White tusks, as sharp as any razor, caught the dancing auras of light from the mass of eggs as it raised a damp snout and snuffled. Below the neck the thing looked superficially like a human, although there were rolls of pink fat in places, and taut sinew and muscle in the shoulders and arms, arms that came to an end not in hands, but in coarse, cloven hooves. The head was squat, almost round, and covered in wiry stubble of coarse hair. Stumpy pointed ears looked too pink, too fleshy. Tiny eyes, like black pearls, were sunk in near shadow above a stubby snout with wide flaring nostrils and those evil tusks, a foot long each, curved back on themselves to end in sharp points that looked capable of impaling the strongest flesh. A caustic, stinging stench permeated the air, causing me to gag as and bring tears to my eyes.

"It came forward towards us, snuffling.

"I showed it the iron bar as I stepped backwards, but it did not slow. I felt Bernard grip tight on my left arm, as if seeking reassurance, but I had none to give him at that moment, for I feared taking my eyes off the beast unless it should immediately launch an attack.

"I stepped back farther, intending to make for the stairs. Bernard was aware enough to move with me, but so too did the beast, coming forward as we retreated. We went on this way for four or five steps in a formalized dance, and I thought we might indeed be able to make the relative safety of the stairs when Bernard gasped.

"Mr. Carnacki, there is another, to your left."

"I saw a darker shadow move out of the corner of my eye at the same time as the evil stench got stronger than ever. My next action was pure instinct, and Arkwright would have been proud of the stroke. I stepped forward as if receiving a slower ball on a bouncing wicket and swung the cold iron like a cricket bat, right at the damnable swine-thing's head.

"I hit nothing more substantial than cold air and dust, but the beast fell apart as if thunderstruck. At the same instant the mass of eggs throbbed, once, and there was an explosion of color and rainbow aurora that dashed near blinded me. I had enough presence of mind to drag young Bernard with me and made for the stairs with all haste.

"A minute later we were back up in the hallway, standing inside the pentacle, our heads reeling as we tried to make some sense out of what had occurred."

★

Carnacki paused in his tale, and indicated it was time for a fresh, or rather, a last, charge of our glasses.

"We are at the crux of the matter now, chaps," he said,

"and I am unlikely to want to stop again before the tale is done, so fill your glasses and get some smokes lit. We have to stand in the dark with young Bernard for a time and see him off on his chosen path."

Arkwright looked like he, as usual, had questions, but his earlier blunder in interrupting the story had clearly made him more circumspect now, for he held his peace for once, and it was only minutes before we were all back in our chairs gathered around the fireplace.

Carnacki wasted no time in continuing.

★

"After I ensured that young Bernard was not going collapse into a blue funk, I left him smoking a cigarette and set to switching on the pentacle. It was still only late afternoon, and there was as yet plenty of light coming in the window above the door. But after what we had seen, I felt the desire to be as well protected as I possibly could, despite the threat of the battery not being able to last the distance.

"I took one further precaution. I remembered how the act of modulating the washes of color from the valves had influenced the veil in our previous encounters, so I included in my setup the small rack of switches and dials with which I have most recently been experimenting. I had no idea whether they would prove of any use at all, but it was surely better to have all the tools at my disposal in play.

"I finished my preparations only just in time. In our haste to get back to the pentacle, we had left the door to the basement swinging open, and now the sound from inside there was clear. There was a recurrence of the snuffling, sniffing noise, and a thud, as of heavy footsteps on the stairs.

"We were about to have company."

★

"I switched on the pentacle. Color washed around the hallway in swirls of blue and green, yellow and red, but the shadows in the cellar doorway stayed resolutely dark and black.

"Bernard bent and lifted the iron bar from where I had

left it beside the defenses box, but I put a hand on his arm.

"'Stay your hand, lad. We're playing by my rules now,' I said. 'We will be protected inside the circles. Now is not the time for hasty action. Lets us calm ourselves, and see what there is to be seen. We might have a long night ahead of us.'

"He lowered the bar, but kept it hanging in his left hand as he smoked. I got my pipe lit, as the smell of animal came again, and the black shadows swirled in the doorway to the basement. Another shadow grew, back up on the landing at the top of the first flight of stairs, and as that one took form, so too did the one in the doorway solidify and come forward. There was another at its back, and another after that.

"It was only a matter of a minute before we had half a dozen of the stocky swine things in the hallway with us, all circling the pentacle, sniffing and snuffling and snorting. Each looked the double of the other. There was nothing to tell them apart, save possibly that the one that came first up the stairs had a slightly larger head and a longer set of tusks. I took note of the fact that they all appeared to shy away when they got closer to the front door, as if disturbed by the extra light coming in there from above. I bent to my box of tricks and turned the power up in the yellow valve, which immediately flared brighter.

"The response was immediate. The beasts backed away, both from the doorway, and from the brightly shining valve, and now cowered in a tight bunch by the stairwell, as if unsure of their next move. To be on the safe side, I turned up all the valves. The battery would drain all the faster for it of course, but whatever I was doing, it was working for the moment.

"Then I made a mistake. I pushed the power up farther, and at the same time set the valves to pulse, rotating the brightness in phases through the colors, sending washes of blue and yellow and green all through the hallway. But I had been too hasty. I should have rested on my laurels, for the washing color, instead of repelling the swine things, only served to enrage them and, as one, they charged forward and threw themselves at our defenses.

"Now at this point, of course, Arkwright would have taken up the cold iron and leapt into the fray swinging. But he is made of sterner stuff than I, and I stood, side by side with my young friend, as the beasts charged against the wall being provided by the pentacle and the circles.

"Light blazed and sparked from the valves as the swine things attacked, again, and again, heads down like squat bulls, testing their horns against the defenses.

"Bernard's knuckles went white where he gripped the cold iron, and I saw the nervous tension build in him as the attacks grew ever more frenzied. But the pentacle held, and the beasts finally relented and retreated once more into their huddle by the foot of the stairs, as if intent on conversing on a fresh course of action.

"I took the opportunity to return the valves to sending out soft washes rather than pulses of color, and that did indeed take much of the tension out of the situation. The beasts went quiet and still, and took to a watching brief.

"It appeared that we had reached an impasse."

★

"I must admit that young Bernard was taking matters with rather more aplomb and calm that I might have expected. He was indeed tense, but then, so was I. When he put the iron bar down on top of the box and lit a fresh cigarette there was no discernible tremble in his fingers.

"I was about to compliment him on his manner when I noted he was not looking at me, nor at the swine things at the foot of the stairs, but over my shoulder, toward the doorway of room number one. I turned to check on what had caught his eye.

"There appeared to be sunlight coming under the bottom of the door, but where the light in the window above the main doorway was thin and watery as late afternoon turned toward evening, this was golden, warm and inviting. I could almost feel the heat from it.

"'She is here,' Bernard whispered. He stubbed out his cigarette and clasped the locket he wore tight in his palm. "She is waiting for me."

"He started to move. I grabbed hard at him, preventing him from leaving the circle.

"'You cannot know that. It might be a fresh trick to lull us into a false sense of security.'

"He brushed me aside. He had the advantage both in youth and strength and was able to break away from me easily. He bent and lifted the iron bar again, letting it swing in his left hand.

"'In this matter, you must trust me, Mr. Carnacki. As you have seen the veil before, so I have seen this. This is what was shown to me in Paris, and it is the very reason I am standing here now. My lady awaits me. I must go to her.'

"Before I could do any more to stop him, he stepped out of the circle and over to the door. I expected the swine things to attack at that moment, but they were reluctant to leave the shadows. They even appeared to cower back farther toward the stairs, as if in fear of Bernard. They fell strangely quite and docile, and became even more so when he opened the door and warm sunlight poured out into the hallway from the apartment beyond.

"Bernard spoke, his voice low and soft so that I did not catch his words. And from the room beyond the door, somebody replied, a woman's voice, high and musical. I could not catch her words either, but she sounded almost heart-aching happy.

"The young Frenchman walked into the room and closed the door softly behind him. Sunlight still showed underneath it, but there was no sound, and I was left alone in the hallway with the group of swine things glowering at me from the shadows at the foot of the stairs."

★

"I stood there for the time it took me to smoke a pipe of tobacco, wondering whether I could not have done more to prevent Bernard's rash action, and wondering whether he had even now gone to his doom. There was no sound apart from the occasional snuffle from the beasts, but they appeared to be calmed by the washes of color from the pentacle and showed no inclination to mount another attack. I was however worrying about the drain on my battery. This was the smaller of the pentacles, but it was powered the oldest and least powerful battery that I had.

"I was watching the valves carefully for any sign of

dimming when the door of number one opened again, and Bernard came back out into the hallway."

★

"Something had changed in the lad. He looked straighter in the back, much more composed and assured in his manner, and the air of doom and melancholy he had carried with him since we met was completely lifted from his shoulders. When one of the swine things dared to snuffle and grunt, he strode quickly across the hallway, past the pentacle, and got into them with the iron bar with great swinging sweeps to his left and right.

"He wielded the iron as if it were weightless, using it not like a bat as I had earlier, but rather like a great knight of renown would wield a sword. The swine things wailed and snuffled piteously, but there was no escape from the cold iron. They fell apart into shadow and dust at his feet.

"When Bernard turned back to me, he had a broad smile on his face.

"I believe it is safe for you to leave your defenses, Mr. Carnacki. The deal is done and my path is set before me. This is my place now. I am home."

"I heard a giggle, almost girlish, from room number one, then the door swung shut. I stepped out of the pentacle and went over to open it again, hoping to see what he had seen, but the sunlight had gone, and there was once again only another empty apartment beyond."

★

"I was loath to leave it at that. The sun was going down behind the castle outside and it would soon be night again, but young Bernard looked forward to it with something that looked like joy to me.

"'I shall never leave here again,' he told me. 'But if you please, could you leave your box of defenses with me? They may prove useful. I do not think the swine things will bother me now that I am master of the house, but it would be best to be prepared in any case. I have seen how your pentacle is used, and I promise to be in touch should I have any problem I cannot handle.'

"I, in turn, promised to have a word with my sergeant and get him to inform the renovator that he had a buyer for his property. I did not think there would be any problems or delay with Bernard getting his wish to proceed with the purchase with all haste.

"I spent several minutes reassuring myself that I was not going to be leaving the lad in a tight spot, then I bid him goodbye, and went back to the North British, where I had a fine supper and slept like a baby.

"In the morning, I did as I had promised and visited the police station where I spoke to the sergeant and told him that his 'bogle' was gone and, better still, the house had a prospective buyer. He was mightily relieved and thanked me profusely for my efforts.

"On checking out of the hotel, I found that I had a couple of hours to spare before the next train south so I went down to the Grassmarket to check on Bernard and ensure he had survived the night none the worse for wear.

"I did not speak to him, but as I approached the townhouse, I saw him at the doorstep welcoming an elderly lady clad entirely in black. I was close enough to hear his words.

"'Yes, I am the new concierge," he said. "And all who suffer are welcome here. I have number one, but number three is free, should you wish it.'

"I turned away before he could see me, and made my way slowly back to the hotel to pack for home."

★

It took us several seconds to realize that Carnacki's tale was over.

"But what about the bally swine things?" Arkwright almost bellowed.

Carnacki smiled.

"It is probable they are still there, beyond the veil. But Bernard is the master of the house now, and they know it. They will keep their distance, and if they do not, well, he has the pentacle."

"But damn and blast it, Carnacki," Arkwright continued, "this is a rum do; a rum do indeed. Do you mean to tell us you now believe in some form of an afterlife?"

"Not quite," Carnacki replied. "But let us say that I believe that nothing is ever truly lost. There are always possibilities. And when the alternative is the implacable, uncaring, immensity of the void that is the Outer Darkness, then perhaps some comfort can be found in that."

He ushered us to the door and sent us out into the night.

"Now, out you go," he said.

A Night in the Storeroom

For once, I arrived in Cheyne Walk ahead of schedule, and was first to be shown in by my good friend, Carnacki. To my eye, he looked tired, and more than that, he looked fatigued, as if he had been under a great strain of some kind. He waved away my attempt at an amateur medical diagnosis.

"I'm well enough, thank you, Dodgson," he replied. "It's nothing some good company, a hearty supper, and a few glasses of scotch won't cure."

But when he smiled, it did not quite reach his eyes. Indeed, he was so worn out I did not expect a story from him that night, but after the others arrived he perked up. Arkwright monopolized much of the conversation over our meal of steak and fried potatoes, but Carnacki was by no means silent, and at least had some color in his cheeks as he bade us gather round the fire in the parlor to hear of his latest exploits.

But it was as well that it was a quiet night in the street outside, for our friend's voice had lost much of its usual depth and timbre, and at times he barely rose above a whisper. We soon forgot that, however, for as ever, he proved to be a fine storyteller, and we were quickly lost in his tale, gripped as ever by his latest adventure.

★

"My story this week begins in the quietest of places, and ends with a bang," he began. "It all started last Monday. You will remember it was a dreary, miserable kind of day, with low gray skies and interminable drizzle. I was doing my best to avoid the weather, and had been spending the morning in the quiet of the British Museum Library with a table piled high with musty old books. As you can imagine, I was as happy as a pig at a trough.

"My most recent research has been centered on the history and legends in the immediate localities around Grimes Graves and it is turning into a deep, and fascinating area of study. I am sure that there will be a Friday night story or two arising from it in the months to come for you chaps to enjoy. But for now, that is a secondary matter and is not pertinent to the story at hand. I was lost in a medieval transcript of a Roman consul's letters to the Senate when I felt someone arrive at my shoulder.

"I was still looking downward at the books, so I saw his legs and feet first. I knew who it was before I turned and looked up, for the librarian, old Charles Masterson, always wears his carpet slippers in the library, in order that he can pad around while still maintaining the silence necessary for allowing scholars peace and quiet in which to study.

"When he spoke to me, it was in the most quiet whisper he could manage, and even then he looked as if the noise itself pained him.

"'Excuse me, Mr. Carnacki, sir. But may I have a word? In the vestibule?'

"I saw by the look on his face that the matter was of a serious nature so I left my books on the table and followed the old chap out. My own footsteps were not so muffled as his, and I drew some glares and pained glances for my trouble before I got safely out from under the echoing dome.

"'I am dashed sorry to disturb you, sir,' old Masterson said once we were out in the main hall with the heavy library door shut behind us. 'But as you know, I am familiar with your areas of study, and I believe you might be able to do the museum a great service, if you are so inclined?'

"As you can imagine, he had now caught my attention. I lit up a smoke, and motioned that he should continue. He lowered his voice and leaned in close so that he would not be overheard, although there was no one else in the hallway but we two.

"'We've got a haunt, sir,' he said. 'Well not here, not in the library, although some nights I hear things here too. But that's merely sounds, and whispers in the rafters. No, it's in the museum's main storerooms where the problem is. And it's more than sounds; things are moved around at night when nobody is watching, and there's a smell too, so I've heard. I've never noticed anything myself of that nature you understand, but I've heard the tales from men that I know are not prone to flights of fancy.

"'It's got so that the staff won't go down there alone any more, and rumors are spreading. And these are all members of staff who've been here for years, some nearly as long as I have myself. They're not flighty chaps looking for a pay rise. I've been told all of this in confidence, but I'm afraid the tales might spread. And what if the public, or even, God forbid, the newspapers got wind of it? The museum's good name is at stake here, Mr. Carnacki, and I know you are a man who values tradition and history. Can you help us?'

"It had all come out from him in a rush, as if he had been bottling it up in readiness for this occasion. His worried fretting, and the way he bowed and scraped and wrung his hands made the old chap seem rather comical, but I refrained from smiling, for he appeared to be genuinely distressed. And he had aided me many a time in my quests for ancient tomes on dusty shelves. I could do little else but to return the favor, at least in going as far as to hear him out and get the full detail of the story.

"So it was that, after returned it the library and retrieving my notes and satchel, I was led off into the museum proper than down, via a series of stairwells and brickwork passages, into the storerooms below the main building."

★

"By Jove, lads, there are treasures there the like of which I have never before clapped eyes on. The history of our civilization is all laid out, some of it in full view and gathering dust, other parts stacked in a maze of crates that stretched away as far as the eye can see into a gloomy distance. I saw statues and paintings and carvings and suits of armor and huge sarcophagi built of blocks of granite, so heavy that must have taken scores of men days to move into their position. One could be down there for many years, lifetimes even, and one would only begin to uncover the wonders to be seen. But I had no time to tarry. Old Masterson was already hurrying me on, leading me ever deeper into the stacks.

"The whole storeroom was rather gloomy. There are electric light fittings, but not quite enough bulbs to do the job properly, and those that it does have are set high in rows in the ceiling, and ran some ten feet above our heads. They glowed little brighter than a candle might have done, and only provided the most basic of illumination.

"'Are you sure you know where you're going, old chap?' I asked after we had dodged left and right several times in what was becoming a proper warren.

"'Almost there,' he replied, and kept going.

"After several more minutes, and a few more twists and turns, we rounded a corner past an enormous, and exceptionally grotesque statue of a grimacing lion with an eagle's wings, and I nearly walked into Masterson's back when he stopped abruptly in front of me.

"'Oh, my dear Lord,' he whispered, the sound echoing around and about us.

"'Is there a problem, Masterson?'

"'Oh, my dear Lord,' he said again.

"I had to peer over his shoulder to see what had stopped him. The crates at this point were spread apart leaving a twelve-feet on a side clearing in the maze. They were also stacked high, three or four on top of another, so that it almost felt like we stood at the entrance to a narrow canyon. And there, right in the center of the empty area, a body was spread-eagled on the floor.

"The chap was clearly dead. His eyes, pale as milk, stared sightlessly at the dim bulbs that looked down at him from the ceiling. But, of course, I had to check. I pushed Masterson aside and went to bend over the body.

"There was no sign of any foul play, but the poor chap looked like he had died in abject terror. He had his left hand gripped across his chest, balled into a fist, and his lips were pulled back from this teeth in a grimace. He had bitten into his tongue, and blood filled his mouth. I have seen dead men before, but never one that looked to have had such a hard time in the passing.

"Masterson hadn't yet moved an inch, and the old chap

could not take his eyes from the body.

"'It's John Jennings, isn't it?' he said.

"'I wouldn't know,' I replied. 'But I take it you know the man?'

"Masterson was still staring at the body.

"'I've known him for years. He's the curator of the Grecian exhibits. He must have been down here looking for something and…'

"He didn't finish the sentence. All color had leeched from his face, and he looked like he might be about to collapse in a dead faint. I realized that I had to get his mind onto a subject other than the dead chap at my feet.

"'Fetch a policeman,' I said, then had to repeat myself, for he clearly wasn't listening.

"'And where would I find one?' he finally replied.

"'Go out into the street and shout,' I said, with a tad more exasperation than I probably should have shown. 'One will find you, if you yell loudly for long enough.'

"The old chap left at a run as if pleased to have been given leave to depart. I heard the soft pad of his footsteps head away into the stacks, then I was left there alone in the dimly lit storeroom, in the quiet.

"I was suddenly only too aware that there was a dead body at my feet."

★

"It did not take too long for the quiet to start to work on me as I stood there in the silence and gloom. I knew, of course, that I could follow Masterson and walk out at any time, but somehow I felt that if I left now, I would be doing a disservice to the poor dead chap below me.

"Besides, I had completely failed to take note of the twists and turns by which I had been led here, and blundering around in the maze of stacks in the gloom did not appeal to me in the slightest. I stepped away from the body and leaned against a wall of crates while I got a pipe lit.

"The simple mechanics of lighting up a smoke going did much to steady my nerves. But the only noise after that was any that I made myself; the suck of my lips on the pipe's stem or the hissing of tobacco leaf as it burned. The smoke I produced hung around me rather than dispersing. The fug hovered and swirled like an angry rain cloud, mere feet above my head, and it spread out below the closest of the light bulbs, thick enough to be casting everything in a dim gray glow.

"My brain started to give me ideas and unwanted thoughts of what might have brought the chap on the floor to his fate. In trying to avoid thinking about that, I only stirred up memories of my own, those born from standing alone for too long in dark places.

"I strained to hear any sound that might tell me there was another worker down here in the dark, a curator or a janitor or a delivery man, I cared not who it might be, as long as they were keeping me a distant company. But there was only a dead, seemingly muffled, silence.

"And then I heard it.

"It was no more than a quiet sniff at first, like someone trying to clear his nasal passages. I thought that my wish for company had been granted, and I called out.

"'Hello?'

"I was answered by a shriek that I took to be a bat at first but proved to be the squeal of a crate being moved aside on the floor. It was not too close by, but the quiet of the storeroom amplified every sound tenfold.

"'Hello?' I said again.

"This time I got another sniff in reply, and this one was a dashed sight closer than the first. I can tell you I was soon in a bally blue funk, and I am not afraid to admit it.

"There was yet another sniff, more of a snuffle this time, as if something was testing the air, seeking a smell. I had the sudden feeling that I might be the one who was being sought, and when the air moved, as if something heavy was creeping around on the other side of the crate on which I was leaning, I finally had enough.

"As I started to walk away, I smelled something, thick and cloying, animalistic and heavy, like a dog that's rolled in a cowpat. Then it snuffled again, and the crate at my back trembled, as if a weight were leaning against it.

"I took to my heels."

★

At this point Arkwright interrupted. I'm afraid that the poor chap was unable to contain his outburst.

"Tell me now, Carnacki. Is it those blasted swine things again? For if it is, I shall retire to the dining room for a quiet smoke on my own and leave you chaps to it. I cannot abide to hear of them again. The bally things haunt my dreams enough as it is."

Carnacki smiled thinly.

"No, old friend," he said. "You can safely stay in your seat. I can assure you that it was not swine that haunted the Museum storeroom that night; although, like you, those beasts haunt my own dreams, and were the first thought that came to my mind even as I fled."

★

"I ran through the stacks, full pelt, aware that I had not the slightest clue where I was headed, but also aware that something followed me, at every twist and turn, something large, heavy enough to brush crates aside as it came. It was closer. I smelled it again, stronger now, a powerful stench of an animal on the hunt, but any time I chanced a look back I saw nothing but the alley of crates through which I was currently running.

"Even above my hurried footsteps, and the rasp of my own breath, I heard another snuffle, and a louder grunt, almost at my back now. I put on a spurt of speed, taking a quick left, then right. I was looking backward, anticipating an attack and not really paying too much attention to the way I was going.

"I ran into something warm, and let out a panicked yelp, thinking the thing that was after me had somehow got in my way. I struggled for an instant, then felt strong arms grip at my shoulder.

"'I say. It's Carnacki, isn't it? What the blazes are you doing here, man?'

"When I was able to catch my breath, I looked at the man who had grabbed me. Now that I was no longer in such a funk, I recognized him immediately. It was Whittaker,

Inspector Whittaker of the Yard, the same inspector who had brought me the case of the Egyptian Scarab I related to you some months back. And to say I felt jolly foolish to have been so startled to meet him would be somewhat of an understatement. At that moment, I could not think of a single word to say in reply to him.

"Masterson was standing behind the inspector, and it was the old librarian who spared my blushes.

"'Mr. Carnacki is a long time friend of the museum, sir,' he said, 'and he was with me when I found the body.'

"'Was he indeed?' Whittaker replied, and gazed keenly at me, as if trying to discern any culpability in my being there. He saw nothing untoward, and turned back to Masterson. 'Well then, lead on. We can't be traipsing around here in the murk all day. Where's this bally body of yours?'

"I was dismissed, and once again I had an opportunity to beat a hasty retreat should I have wished to. But I felt dashed sheepish and not a small bit ashamed at my panic of moments earlier, so I gave myself a stern talking to, and followed as Masterson led the inspector deeper into the stores."

★

'There was a small troupe of us as we returned through the stacks, Masterson, Whittaker, a doctor, Whittaker's sergeant, two constables, and me bringing up the rear. I was alert to any small sound, and sniffed at the air, ready to flee if I smelled the animal again. But now that I was among people again, my previous experience was already fading, taking on an almost dreamlike quality, as if it had happened a long time ago, to someone else rather than myself.

"When we arrived back at the open area where the body was lying, I half-expected the body to have vanished, like in some lurid Penny Dreadful plot, but the poor chap was still there on his back, staring at the ceiling. Masterson could not approach beyond the entrance to the canyon of crates. Nor could he speak; he merely pointed, mutely, at what we could all see in any case.

"It did not take the Yard's doctor long to confirm what I already knew. The man Jennings was as dead as dead can be.

The doctor's diagnosis of heart failure was an obvious one in the circumstances, but I saw Whittaker look over to me, then away again, as if he had something he wanted to ask of me but did not want the others present to hear. His attention was only taken from me when the doctor let out an exclamation.

"'I have something here,'

"He pried something out of the dead man's clenched hand, and passed it to the inspector. Whittaker looked at whatever it was, then back at me again. He raised an eyebrow, but still said nothing."

★

"He finally got a chance to say his piece when the doctor was done, the sergeant and the constables took the body away, and everyone departed the scene but the inspector and myself. We stood over where the body had been lying, and he passed me a cigarette before lighting us both up with a safety match.

"'You think there's more going on here than meets the eye, don't you, Carnacki?'

"I told him of how I had got involved, of Masterson's tales of night haunts and spooks, and I told him of my own experience in that same spot, before running into him as he arrived.

"'It's like that thing you had in your library in Chelsea? Another bally nasty Egyptian serpent?'

"I shook my head.

"'I don't know yet what manner of thing we are dealing with. This feels different to me; it feels a lot stronger. I shall need to spend more time with it to determine its true nature. And for that, I shall need permission to spend the night down here. Old Masterson is unlikely to give it to me, despite my friendship to the museum. I'm not staff, you see.'

"'Permission can be arranged,' Whittaker said softly. 'But surely it is dangerous? Don't you run the risk of coming to the same end as the unfortunate chap we have found?'

"'Rather me than some other poor soul,' I said. I was not sure I meant to sound quite so bally brave about it, but Whittaker took me at my word.

"'Then I shall stand with you,' he replied. 'And perhaps this may help you in your investigation. The dead man had it gripped tight in his hand.'

"He passed the thing that the doctor had given to him over to me. It was a small charm, the kind a lady might hang on a bracelet, although in this case, it would have to have been a rather well off lady. It appeared to be made of solid gold, and it was most finely sculpted. It depicted a heavy-set bull's head, broad, and with wide, arching horns that almost touched each other above a glowering black-eyed stare."

★

"I arranged to meet Whittaker again in the museum vestibule at seven in the evening, and he in turn agreed to arrange the appropriate permissions for the night's vigil. This time, as we made our way out of the storeroom, I remembered to take note of the twists and turns through the stacks, before taking my leave of the inspector on the Museum steps.

"I made my way back here to Chelsea. By the time I had negotiated the traffic, got home, prepared my box of defenses, and arranged for a carriage back to the Museum, it was already almost five. I had time for a quick bite of bread and cold ham, and then I was back out on the street again, and soon making my way north once more.

"Whittaker, as good as his word, was waiting for me at the museum doors. He helped me inside with the box of defenses, and between us we lugged it down through the passageways and through the maze of the stacks, until we were finally able to let it down on the floor in the empty space where we'd found the body.

"I had a break for a smoke before starting with the preparations; even with the inspector's help it had been quite an effort to lug the kit down, and I was not in the slightest looking forward to the return journey. It felt like it had been a long day already, and I had a feeling I had a way to go yet before I would be granted any real respite."

★

"None of the sounds of the great city above penetrated down to us and, surrounded as we were by the relics of antiquity, it felt as if we were completely cut off from the modern world and had been dropped down into a point of some remote history. However, such musings were not doing anything for my nervous disposition, so I finished my smoke quickly and got to setting up the defensive circles.

"Whittaker had not seen this part of the process, having previously only encountered the circles I have inlaid on the library floor, so he was most attentive as I made the lines in chalk. He was also full of questions about the why and wherefore of the protections, the answering of which slowed me considerably. I was forced to get a move on when I heard the first snuffling and grunting come from somewhere out in the darkness of the stacks.

"Once I got the chalk work done I had the inspector step inside the circles to the center of the pentacle. He did so with a smile and a raise of an eyebrow that told me that, despite my explanations as to the need for protection, he was, as yet, not taking this quite so seriously as I would have liked. But I had run out of time to educate him otherwise; a grunt came out in the stacks. I smelled it again; the heavy, musky odor of some huge beast, as out of place among these crates and artifacts as I was myself.

"I laid out the electric valves along the peaks and troughs of the pentacle and, carrying the battery and my control system with me, stepped inside the circles to join Whittaker. I switched on the pentacle, and in the nick of time it seemed. The red valve surged into brightness faster than the others, and looked to be aflame as it sent a fiery wash of color over the surrounding crates.

"There was another grunt, louder than ever, and a snuffle, followed by a high screech as crates were roughly shoved aside as if they were empty cardboard boxes. The red flared again and something took shape in front of us, something huge. Something monstrous."

★

"I knew the manner of the beast almost straight away,

for the head showed first, thin and vaporous to start with, but quickly becoming clearer to show the head, shoulders and horns of a great black bull. In proportion it appeared to be identical to the gold charm that Whittaker even now held in his palm.

"The head might have resembled a great bull, but below the shoulders was a different matter entirely. A mat of course hair hung around its thick, tree-trunk neck, but it sat above the broad expanse of an all too human chest, albeit one that was as broad as a barrel and corded in tight bunches of muscle that looked to be as solid as rock. There was more coarse hair at the waist, thick enough to make it seem like more of a roughly made kilt, and the legs beneath that looked more bovine than anything human. But it had no trouble standing upright to its full height. I had to raise my gaze to look at the head again, it being almost eight feet tall at a guess.

"And if it wasn't a bally Minotaur, then I will eat my hat.

"It came forward towards the defensive circles, slowly, as if unsure about the color that washed around us. The stench got stronger still, almost overpowering. Whittaker, cool as you like, lit up a smoke to mask the smell, and I joined him, lighting a fresh pipe, all the while not taking an eye off the beast.

"It raised the great head and grunted again, then began pawing at the air. It was only then that I noticed it had no hands to speak of. The wrists each ended in huge, cloven hooves, both of them the size of heavy hammers. Even as I had the thought, the thing stepped forward, right up next to the outermost circle, and struck down, hard, as if intending to deal both of us inside a killing blow. Instead, the defenses shrieked in a howl that almost deafened me, and the red valve flared, as bright as the sun itself.

"The Minotaur wailed as if in some distress, and retreated. We heard the clatter of hooves on the stone slabs of the floor, and a distant grunting, then the storeroom fell deathly quiet again."

★

"'That went well,' Whittaker said, deadpan, and with so little intonation that I was unsure whether I should be detecting a note of sarcasm. 'Is it over?'

"I shook my head.

"'I fear the night has only begun to show us its surprises,' I replied. I pointed out to the gap in the crates. Something was taking shape there, not the Minotaur, but something else entirely, a wispy, almost smoky figure, bipedal and upright, much more human in form than the beast we had scared off.

"'What in blazes is that? Please tell me that is not a bally ghost.' Whittaker said, and this time I definitely heard the intonation in his voice, only it wasn't sarcasm; this time it was a touch of something very much like terror.

"Whatever the blazes it was, it certainly looked human, and it walked around the perimeter of the defenses without ever reaching close enough to affect the brightness of the valves. At its closest approach I saw that it was wrapped in a swaddling robe, in many ways resembling a desert nomad, a hood hanging forward obscuring any features. It made no sound, and hardly touched the floor at all; it appeared to glide, as if mounted on silent wheels, and kept circling, so fast that I was becoming quite dizzy while following its progress.

"Whittaker put a hand on my shoulder and turned me round to face the opening in the crates. I immediately saw what had got his attention. The Minotaur was back, not yet fully formed but more a huge, bull-shaped area of mist and shadow that came forward quickly and loomed over the robed figure.

"There was no sound when the attack came. The Minotaur raised a cloven hand, and brought it down hard on the spectral robes. The human shaped figure came apart into not much more than dust and shadow and the Minotaur took a huge, deep, breath. It sucked in everything that remained of the spectral, figure, dark and shadow and mist and all.

"The red valve flared brighter, the Minotaur grunted and sniffled, and backed off again to hide itself somewhere in the stacks.

"But it was obvious to me, and also I guessed to Whittaker.

"The bally thing had got bigger, and more solid after eating."

★

"'What happened?' Whittaker whispered, as if afraid to raise his voice.

"'I was wondering that myself, old boy,' I replied. 'I believe we have witnessed a strong manifestation from the Outer Darkness subsuming a weaker form.'

"'In English, please, Carnacki?'

"'I think that the artifacts in this storeroom have been accumulating passengers over millennia, small fragments of the outer dark that coalesce and clump together and, sometimes, gain enough cohesion to take form. The longer the accumulation has been taking place, the stronger the resultant manifestation.'

"'Yes, that's certainly cleared things up for me,' Whittaker said, and this time I did indeed hear the sarcasm, loud and clear.

"'I do not have the time in one night to explain thousands of years of arcane philosophy,' I said. 'But trust me on this if nothing else, we must stay in the circles at all cost, for yon bull, call it Minotaur, or manifestation, if you prefer, is strong. And it is obviously hungry."

★

"I had spoken off the cuff, making up a theory on the spot, but as the evening and then nighttime progressed it became clear that my first surmise had been a good one.

"The robed figure proved to be only the first apparition to reveal itself. Others came, as if drawn to the pentacle like moths to a flame. Some were no more than mere wisps of smoke and shadow, others were firmer, older, and with more intent. Whittaker almost took a funk when a long, worm-like thing with too many legs scuttled toward us out of the darkness and looked like it might leap clean over the valves. But the defenses held, the yellow flared, and even as the thing fell away, repulsed, the Minotaur was there at its rear to bring up a cloven hand, and smash the worm into motes of sparkling dust that it once again breathed deep into itself.

"And now there was no mistaking it; the bally thing was definitely becoming more solid.

"It was also becoming emboldened. After taking in the essence of the worm, the Minotaur tried another assault on the defenses. It threw its not inconsiderable bulk against the outer circle, again and again. The red valve flared brightly, but this time the beast was not so easily frightened off, and it kept pushing forward. The valve whined, straining at its maximum output. It was only when I remembered that I had my control panel with me that I thought to modulate the frequencies and add a pulsing blue and green to the mix. The fresh wash of color confused the beast again, and it backed off, heading back into the gloom of the stacks.

"But once the whine of the over-stretched valves faded back to their normal soft hum, we heard it clear enough. It was still close by, grunting and snuffling on the other side of the crates."

★

"Poor Inspector Whittaker had lost much of his earlier self-assurance, and was ashen-faced when I turned to him. His hands trembled as he tried to light a cigarette.

"'He almost got through to us that time, didn't he?' he asked, still whispering.

"'It was dashed close, I'll give you that,' I said, and in truth, I shared his misgivings. I did not think much of our chances of surviving another such attack.

"The Minotaur returned as I was lighting a fresh pipe, but this time did not come close to the circles. Instead it was intent on pursuing another new apparition, a dark patch of shadow that flitted and danced across the crates but was no match for the bull's strength and power. It too was sucked up by one enormous breath that caused the barrel chest to swell and tighten.

"More darkness swirled above us in the roof space, and again I thought of the moth to a flame analogy. Another thought struck me, one that I wished had stayed away, but the more I thought about it, the more I knew that it was our only chance of getting out of this situation intact. I told Whittaker of my thinking, hoping that by speaking it aloud I might uncover a flaw in my argument.

"'The pentacle is clearly acting as an almost magnetic source for these apparitions. All we are doing is bringing more food in for the bally beast,' I said.

"Whittaker nodded.

"'I have already noticed that. But we cannot turn it off, can we? We will only leave ourselves open to immediate attack.'

"'I have a plan,' I replied. 'What if I increase the valves' brightness and bring every bally denizen of the darkness here, all at once. What if we let the beast gorge itself to its heart's content?'

"'How does that help us?' Whittaker asked.

"'That's the tricky bit,' I replied.

"'I'm not sure I'm going to like this, but go on.'

"'We feed it everything there is to give to it.'

"'Yes, you said that already. But what do we do then, Carnacki? What happens when it has had its fill?'

"'Then we attack.'"

★

"There was little point in wasting time. Thankfully, Whittaker did not ask me how I meant to mount an attack. There was a great risk involved in the path I meant to undertake, and if I had tried to explain it, it would only have confused, and possibly terrified, the poor inspector further than I had already.

"I puffed on my pipe as I turned the knobs on the control panel to their maximum extent. The valves brightened and their glow became almost overpoweringly bright.

"The response was immediate. Dark shapes, like batwings, swooped and fluttered all around the defenses, fragments of the Outer Darkness torn from their attachment to the artifacts around us, drawn by the elemental light of the pentacle.

"And, as they were drawn close, so too was the great bulk of the Minotaur. It rampaged around the outside of the circles, stomping and grunting and pawing, inhaling great breaths that whooped like a rush of wind. And with each breath, it consumed and enveloped more darkness, and became larger, ever more solid.

"Within five short minutes it appeared to have ingested every scrap of dancing darkness there had been around us.

"It raised up to its full height, ten feet now if it was an inch, and roared, a great bellow that shook dust from the ceiling above and set the rows of dim lit bulbs to swinging. Without further ado, it lowered its head, pointed those huge horns right at my chest, and charged."

★

"The hooves thudded on the floor like hammers on rock, and the bull bellowed as it came, a roar the like of which I hope you chaps never have to endure. It was all I could do to stand my ground. My knees damned near buckled under me but Whittaker, stout chap, held us both up, and we faced the beast as it hit the defenses straight on.

"The red valve flared so bright I had to close my eyes, but even then I heard the high whine of the stressed crystals, and felt pressure build as the Minotaur put its back into the effort of pushing through to get at us.

"'If you really do have a plan, then now's the time, old man,' Whittaker said, suddenly remarkably calm in the face of the threat before us.

"I drew what strength I could from his solidity and stood straight, looking the beast in the eye. It stared back at me. I saw little of any intelligence there, only black, implacable, rage and hunger.

"I threw the switches to turn off the pentacle and the beast bellowed in triumph as we were left, helpless, before it. It brought up a huge hoofed hand to strike at me, and I played my last card.

"I shouted out words that should never be uttered save in the utmost extremes. I uttered the eight signs, and the last words of power, of the dreaded Saaamaaa Ritual.

"At the same instant that the great bull bellowed and the cloven hand descended a thunderclap blew through the storeroom.

"Crates and pentacle and Whittaker and myself were tossed asunder by a wind that came out of nowhere and blew the bally Minotaur into scraps of darkness that were sent scuttling and flying away, being shredded into ever smaller scraps as they were taken.

"There was one last bellow of rage and frustration, but the wind took that too as it faded, and we were left, lying amid broken statues and shattered crates and the scattered remnants of what had been my best pentacle.

"But we were alive. We had survived."

★

"Dawn was coming up when we eventually dragged ourselves out of the storeroom and upstairs into the museum itself. We had a smoke out on the front steps as the sun's first rays hit the high dome of the library.

"Old Masterson scuttled across the cobbles towards us. I let Whittaker explain the situation and apologize for the mess we had left down below. For my part, I contented myself with assuring the old librarian that the museum should now be back to what passed as normality. The darkness had been fragmented, and it should be many years, certainly beyond my lifetime, before it will coalesce enough to pose any further threat.

"'So it is safe?' Masterson asked, having clearly not understood a word I had said.

"I nodded in reply.

"'Don't go adding any new exhibits from Crete for a while though, there's a good chap.'

"I promised Whittaker that I'd give him a full explanation of what we'd been through over a pie and a pint in the near future, then caught a carriage home. I had enough energy to drag myself to bed, and slept for the best part of sixteen hours.

"I do believe I shall sleep for sixteen more once you chaps are off and on your way home."

★

Carnacki stopped, his tale done, and for once there did

not seem to be much need for any questions.

"I'm glad it wasn't those bloody swine things again," Arkwright said as Carnacki showed us the door.

"As was I, old friend," Carnacki replied. "As was I. Now out you go."

Into the Light

From the personal journal of Thomas Carnacki, 472 Cheyne Walk, Chelsea.

I have thought long and hard about whether I should even transcribe the details of this last week in my journal at all. The implications of what I encountered both in the room under the inn and in the Kensington townhouse, are staggering for the occult and religious history of all us all.

Not only that, but there is a definite potential for misuse of this knowledge by the unscrupulous, such that it might be for the best if I remained silent and let the affair be forgotten to history for now.

And yet, science often progresses through the study of what once might have been called magic. It is surely only a matter of time before a curious professor, or even an enthusiastic amateur, uncovers the principle I have stumbled upon, and opens a door that should forever stay closed to us.

Perhaps then, it is for the best that I relate my tale, even if only to interject the proper amount of caution and as a salutary warning for those who might follow. One thing is absolutely certain though; this note must be solely for my own personal record at this juncture; the rest of the chaps will never hear of this around the fire of a Friday night in Cheyne Walk.

Mr. Churchill was most clear on having me give my promise of that.

★

It begins with another of my, thankfully infrequent, summonses from Winston Churchill. I had not heard much from him since the affair with the German U-Boat in the docks, and that had been fine by me, for my encounters with the First Lord of the Admiralty have usually left me feeling strangely used and unclean. I understand, and will even defend, his right to call me to duty for King and Country, but I do not, and cannot, ever agree with his methods, which are as unscrupulous as they are required.

Last Saturday, although it almost feels like several lifetimes ago, I was surprised by an early morning knock on my front door. I found a burly chap on the doorstep, and from him I took the delivery of a note from Churchill. The note was by way of an introduction to the carrier, Churchill's own carriage driver, and an invitation requesting my presence at an address in Vauxhall that had me racking my brains in trying to work out what manner of premises it might be.

I considered declining, for there were several tasks at hand that I needed to be about. But the request had come from Churchill; I knew that it would be utterly hopeless to try to turn him down, for the man is like a bulldog once he gets his teeth into something. I took enough time to don a jacket and fetch my cheroot case then I was shown into the plush, almost opulent, carriage. As soon as I was inside, away we went, south across the river.

It was only on alighting from the carriage some fifteen minutes later in Vauxhall that I remembered the location. The building, squashed as it was between two rather more modern blocks that towered over it, housed an inn of some antiquity that I had frequented several times in my younger days, although my last visit must have been some twenty years ago.

I remembered there had been some kind of a fuss when *The White Stag* closed its doors for good ten or eleven years back. The details were fuzzy in my memory, but there had been a scandal of some note. I recalled that much of the detail was withheld from the papers in the interests of national security, but it was rumored among the gossiping classes to have involved several members of parliament, some minor European royalty, ladies of ill repute, and a certain quantity of opium. Arkwright had been rather voluble about it one Friday night when he was in his cups.

I had passed the site several times since its closure as it lies off a busy thoroughfare near the river, but I had never paid it any mind. Previously it had looked exactly like what it was, another empty building going slowly to seed and dereliction. But today there were two more burly lads cut from the same cloth as my driver, both standing at the entrance doors of the old inn, guarding the doorway.

By the way they held themselves, and the air of quiet

menace they exuded, I took them for military chaps, Churchill's men. When I descended from the carriage and walked towards them, they stiffened and grew wary. One wrong word or action from me right then and I might never have returned from my trip to Vauxhall. The men only stood aside and allowed me entry when I showed them the signed note from their superior that I carried with me.

I was not surprised on entering to find that Churchill was waiting inside, in what was left of the old public bar area.

Although the establishment hadn't sold liquor for many years, Churchill was not a man to let a small matter like that stop him in his indulgences. He stood at the bar with a bottle of good single malt scotch on the counter before him and two glasses, both already containing a stiff three-finger measure. He smiled as he saw me.

"Good man, Carnacki. I knew you'd come."

"It is not as if you ever leave me much choice in the matter," I replied as he handed me one of the glasses. He also offered me a thick Cuban cigar, but I declined, and lit up one of my cheroots.

"You can always say no," Churchill said between breaths as he puffed hard on his cigar to get it lit. "I am not an ogre, man."

I have often thought of him more as a shark, striking hard and fast at the first hint of blood in the water, but I decided that wasn't anything I should be saying while he had two bruisers at hand in the doorway. Instead I settled for sipping at the scotch. It was a fine, Speyside malt from one of the smaller distilleries and went down jolly well, but I was paying attention as Churchill finally gave me a reason for requesting my presence.

★

"I am sorry for the cloak and dagger nonsense," Churchill began. "But this is another of those rather sensitive issues that have to be kept jolly quiet. If the general public knew half of what goes on in their name, and right under their bally noses at that, we'd have riots on our hands and bloody anarchy. And then where would we be? No, a certain degree of official secrecy is required for the well being of a nation. And I'm afraid you're going to have to trust me on that score, Carnacki. Take it from one who knows."

He waved a hand around the bar. It had been furnished in the traditional style, with oak seating, long ornate mirrors that were surprisingly still in one piece, sturdy wooden tables, and a long sweeping bar that ran the full length of the long room. It stretched away from us, narrowing as it came to a dark and gloomy rear end wall where the inn backed on to the river.

Everything around us was covered in a thick layer of dust and grime. I saw that Churchill had made the only clean spot visible in the foot wide circle he'd cleared in the dust to make a place to put down the scotch and glasses. I doubted if anyone but Churchill and myself had taken a drink inside the place since the day it was shut down.

"It doesn't look like much now, does it," Churchill said. "But back in the day it was one of the busiest bars on the whole south side of the river. The great and the good used to raise hell here, and I mean that both literally and figuratively. All that changed when the scandal that got it closed down happened. But I fear there might have been something left behind, something that was neglected, and that has since festered.

"There is a thing that I need you to take a look at for me. I hope it is in your line of business, for if it is not, I don't know who I can bally well trust with it otherwise."

Of course, I could not turn him down at that stage, and besides, his last statement had me intrigued. We finished our scotch and he led me to the back end near the rear wall, where I now saw there was an open hatchway that led, via a set of worn stone steps, down into what appeared to be a beer cellar below.

"After you, old chap," Churchill said, and smiled. "And be careful. It's bally filthy down there."

As I descended the steps I got a clue as to what he had meant. There had been a fire in the area under the bar at some point in the past, not recently, but one that had been bad enough to leave a thick layer of ash and soot covering everything. Light came in through a small window high up that was itself smeared with a greasy film of thin soot. The window overlooked the river, and despite the soot was letting in enough light for me to see that I wasn't in a beer cellar after all.

The fire that had left the soot and ash behind had also left remnants of furniture: three long sofas, all halfway burned through, and a squat square table that had been overturned and leaned against the wall.

A roughly circular piece of the floorboards, a yard or so at the widest point had been cleared of ash, and I got my first inkling of why Churchill had asked for my help. I could not see all of it, but there was definitely a magic circle and an interior pentagram drawn there.

But this wasn't one of my protections, far from it. I had seen the like of this before, in books in my library, old books, that dealt with calling up all manner of things to do your bidding. This was a summoning circle, and from the quick look I'd had at it, I had a sinking feeling it wasn't mere necromancy that had been attempted in this room.

Whoever had been at work here was after something rather more sensational. It was clear to me now that they had been involved in a medieval ritual of some infamy; this room had seen an attempt at summoning, and controlling, a demon.

★

Of course, I know there are no such things as demons, there are merely mischief making manifestations from the Outer Darkness. But people who dabble in the esoteric disciplines without any training are wont to see what they expect, and especially those of a religious bent to start with. I had no doubt that this small room here under the bar had seen some excitable people get excited, perhaps even over excited while under the influence of drugs and liquor and the promise of power from the great beyond.

While I'd been examining the circle and arriving at some conclusions as to its nature, Churchill had been watching me.

"First impressions, old boy?" he asked.

"Stuff and nonsense," I replied. "People with more money and liquor than sense looking for an easy thrill, and receiving precisely what they were looking for. It's all parlor games and cheap tricks to rook the gullible. You're a man of the world, Churchill; you know that for yourself."

Churchill nodded.

"I have usually been of the same mind," he replied, "despite having come across several things on my travels over the years that have as yet defied explanation. And, like you, I would put this down to too much liquor, money and high spirits. But there is more to it than that, otherwise I would not have bothered you with it in the first place."

"More?" I said, looking round at the burned remains of the room and the marks on the floor. "What more could there possibly be?"

"Just wait," Churchill replied. He hadn't put out his cigar, and he chewed on it as he spoke. I sensed tension in him, a rare thing to see in a man who was normally so self-assured, and I wondered what might be the cause. Then a cloud went over the sun outside the only window, and I saw exactly what had brought on his uncharacteristic nervousness.

A dark, shadowy figure stood inside the circle on the floor, insubstantial, like something produced by smoke and mirrors. It wasn't quite as tall as a man, more child-like in stature and stance, and one that appeared to be bent and twisted, as if all the bones in its body had been broken, then imperfectly set.

It took several seconds before my eyes adjusted to the growing gloom, and it was only then that I got my first clear look, and saw that it was not human, not even remotely. It was reddish in color, appearing almost as burned as the room in which we stood, and it maintained its balance in the circle with the aid of a pair of large, leathery, wings that stretched out from its shoulders and fanned the stale air around. It stared at me from dark, almost black, eyes and I felt an involuntary shiver run through me.

For all intents and purposes, I was looking into the eyes of a demon.

It did not speak, for which I was grateful, but it stared at me most balefully. It opened and closed small fists, gripping with long, slender fingers, as if it wished it had them affixed around my neck. A tongue flicked from the thin black lips; I did not have time to check if it was forked at the end, for at that moment the cloud moved on outside, the sun reappeared, and the figure in the circle became thin and unsubstantial once again, before fading away completely.

"I do not believe in demons," I said, mostly to reassure myself that I had not, in fact, witnessed what I had seen.

Churchill laughed.

"I don't think he cares, old man."

★

Two minutes later we were back up in the bar, with Churchill pouring me another glass of his excellent scotch, and believe me when I tell you, I bally well needed it, for I had taken quite a fright.

"I didn't believe it myself," Churchill said, still chewing on his cigar as I lit up a fresh cheroot, "but one must trust one's eyes, don't you think? They are about all we bally have at our disposal to try to make sense of what has happened here. Would it help if I told you that I think our friend downstairs has been hanging around down there since the turn of the century?"

I realized he was about to embark on what might pass for an explanation, so I bit my tongue on any questions I might have, and let him continue while I sipped at the scotch.

"As you've probably already surmised, the great and the good used to gather in that room downstairs for their 'special' parties; you know the kind of thing, opiates, women, and general debauchery. The powers that be knew of it of course, but as long as it was kept quiet and nobody was hurt, it was allowed to continue.

"That all changed back in ninety-nine. You remember what it was like back then, Carnacki; the preachers of doom, the end of the world cults, signs in the skies, and more religious claptrap and poppycock than one could shake a stick at. A certain lord of the realm, whose name I should not have to mention, could not get enough of that nonsense, and the parties in the room below took on a darker tone under his guidance.

"He had magicians, spiritualists, kooks, openers of the way, mystics, shaman, druids and even some of the Golden Dawn crowd down there at one time or another. He tried everything he could to get some indication that there was more to life than drink, the poppy and his vices." He paused and chewed on his cigar before continuing. "Well, it looks like he eventually succeeded, don't you think, old boy?"

I wasn't quite ready to answer yet, for I still had too many questions of my own filling my mind.

"Certainly, something has happened down there, and it does appear to have stuck around since the circle was drawn on the floor," I replied cautiously. "And the fire? What happened there?"

Churchill laughed bitterly.

"It seems his lordship was not quite ready to face the result of his little experiment. The story goes that he tried to burn it out and made a right bloody horse's arse of the job. That was in the December of the year. You might remember he was taken ill and removed from society? The blighter is still alive, although his son holds the title now, and his former Lordship is in a sanitarium in Yorkshire. He was burned to red meat over most of his body, and now lives in constant pain, and no little terror. I visited him, last week when this affair came to my notice, but there was not a lick of sense to be had out of him."

If Churchill had any sympathy for the man, there was little showing as he continued.

"Four other poor souls were down in that room when the fire tore through it, and they weren't so lucky. A prominent surgeon, whose name you would know if I mentioned it, and three ladies of the night, all died in the same conflagration, and of course, given his Lordship's involvement, it was all hushed up and kept quiet at the time. The thinking was that the fire had ended the matter once and for all.

"But the old place never recovered its former glories. Nobody would work in the bally inn after the fire. A bad reputation was a permanent stain in this particular case, and the building has been lying empty, as you see here, ever since. It has been allowed to sit here, unnoted and unnoticed for more than ten years. Empty, or so everyone thought."

"Obviously something has changed?"

He laughed again at my question.

"I would say so, old boy, wouldn't you too, now that you've seen it for yourself?"

He went on before I could answer, and in truth, I still didn't know what to make of the whole situation, so I was happy to let him rattle on for a bit longer yet.

"I became aware that the site wasn't as derelict, or empty as had been thought when I started hearing reports of strange happenings in the area a couple of weeks back. As First Lord of the Admiralty, I also oversee the river here and I make sure to keep an eye on all the comings and goings on the water. You would be surprised how a seemingly small matter can end up growing into something that might affect the wellbeing of the nation as a whole. So when I heard of milk going sour along the riverbank in this area, and several cases of young ladies, not all of them fallen, enduring painful miscarriages and stillbirths, I started to investigate. All the stories have led me only to one place, right here, in the burned room below the bar. I came, I saw, and I will bally well conquer, with your help."

He fell quiet at that, and I knew that I now had almost as much information as he had, or at least, as much as he was prepared to tell me.

"I still don't see what you expect of me," I said, although, in truth, I was starting to form a dashed good idea.

"Get rid of it for me, Carnacki," Churchill said. "That's what you do, isn't it? Banish the damnable thing back to where it came from and we can all go for a spot of lunch and a few glasses of wine."

"It may not be quite as simple as that," I replied, to which he laughed again.

"No, it never is with you chaps, is it? But I'm asking anyway, old man. Can you help? For King and Country again?"

I thought of the impossible thing down there in the cellar. I did not for the life of me wish to set eyes on it again. But then I remembered Churchill had spoken of miscarriages, and stillbirths. I would never have peace of mind if I walked away and an unborn child subsequently perished through my indecision or inactivity.

Finally I nodded, and Churchill shook my hand.

"Splendid. I knew I could count on you."

I noticed that Churchill's palm was black with soot, but it was ingrained, and none of it had transferred to my own hand. He wiped his hand idly on his coat, finished his drink, and immediately was on to the next thing that concerned him.

"Right. I have to get back to the House. Matters of state, you know, old boy. There's no rest from them. Keep me informed."

And with that he left me, with half a bottle of scotch on the bar, and a demon waiting for me down in the cellar.

★

I knew that, if I wished to proceed, I would have to go back down into the burned darkness below and investigate further. But the sight of the red, winged thing inside the magic circle had given me quite a turn, and I found it damn near impossible to get my legs to bear me toward the cellar hatch.

In the end, it was the thought of dead children that finally got me moving again, although I did wait until I was sure there was bright sunlight coming in the back window before I walked over and went down the steps.

My first task was to have a better look at the design and layout of the magic circle, or at least as much of it as I could see given that a great deal of it was obscured in soot and ash.

On close examination, I saw that it was exactly the kind of thing I'd expect an enthusiastic amateur to deploy, having been copied line for line from one of the more dubious versions that circulate of *The Clavicle of Solomon*.

Given that dodgy provenance, I was now more than a tad surprised that it had actually succeeded in the task set for it. But there was no denying that a presence had indeed been summoned. I saw it, or insubstantial parts of it at least, every time the sun was dimmed, even slightly, and I was ready for a dash upstairs should it cloud over, for I had no wish to see the full thing again, not until I had proper defenses at my disposal.

As soon as gloom threatened to descend again, I decided I had already seen more than enough, and went quickly back up to the bar, where I polished off another glass of Churchill's scotch, although I limited myself to a short measure.

I had work ahead of me, and I had no idea how long it might take to get the job done to Mr. Churchill's satisfaction.

★

Churchill hadn't quite abandoned me completely to my own devices; he had left his man and carriage at the roadside at my disposal, so I was able to make quick time back to Cheyne Walk. While Churchill's man stayed up at the reins of the carriage at my doorstep, I gathered up what I thought I might require, and fortified myself with a quick late lunch of cold meat, bread and cheese.

The man finally deigned to move from his perch when I got outside and he saw me struggling with my box of defenses. He helped me get it into the carriage, then, a mere thirty minutes after arriving in Chelsea, we were on our way back to Vauxhall.

I used the short journey to quickly peruse my own copy of *The Clavicle of Solomon* that I had brought down off the shelf in the library, but I had remembered correctly, the circles drawn on the floor of the cellar were indeed crude and rudimentary in nature. I believed that any success there had been in the conjuring had come from the force of will of the person who'd made them and used them, rather than from any innate power in the lines themselves.

I put the book away in with my defenses. Alongside the chalk, holy water, garlic and salt and some other provisions, I had brought along my most powerful battery, my newest set of valves, and the little box of tricks for modulating the color washes that I have been experimenting all this past year. I had no idea if they were going to suffice, but they were all that I had at my disposal. I could only hope they were going to be enough for me to fulfil Churchill's faith in my expertise.

I would know soon enough.

★

It was mid afternoon by the time we arrived back outside *The White Stag,* and I was rather dismayed to find that the sky had clouded over to a dull gray that promised to have set in for the duration. The carriage driver helped me lug the box of defenses into the bar area, but that was the limit of his duties, for, still without speaking a word to me, he left me alone in the gathering gloom.

At least I had the scotch for company, but again I

limited to myself to only a small snifter while I smoked a cheroot before getting down to the job. Then I could put it off no longer. I went over to the cellar hatch and carefully went down the stone steps, backwards, easing the box of defenses down behind me.

It was only when I reached the bottom step that I turned to face the center of the room, and the circles. The demon was more solid again now that the sun had gone in. It stood where I had seen it earlier, its gaze still fixed on mine, the leathery wings wafting back and forth, the thin lips raised at the corners in a mocking smile.

"You won't be smiling when I'm done with you," I muttered, with far more bravado than I felt at that moment.

I'd had the good sense to include my small oil lantern in the box of defenses, and when I lit that, its flickering light did much to dispel the image of the demon, leaving it as little more than a hazy outline standing in the circle. I tried to keep my eyes averted from it as I drew circles of my own around the older one it stood inside. Inside that, I transcribed a pentagram as well as I was able, avoiding crossing over the already existing lines.

Then all that was left was to place out the electric pentacle, which I managed to do with no fuss or bother, and thankfully no disturbance from the quiet red figure that watched my every move.

By the time I was finally ready to begin, the light was going from the sky as the sun set somewhere beyond the thick gray clouds. I sat on the second bottom step of the stairs and had another smoke, wishing that I had brought the scotch down into the dark with me. When the small window opposite finally showed there was no light coming in from the outside and that full night had fallen, I put out the small oil lamp and switched on the pentacle.

I had begun.

★

It did not take long for the demon, if that was indeed what it was, to show itself again. It started to come into view almost as soon as I switched off the lamp and the wash of colors from my valves only emboldened it and brought it ever more into solid reality.

I sat on the step and watched it closely, trying to ascertain if it had any sense of purpose or intent, but it was more in the nature of a moving image, albeit a solid one, rather than anything with any degree of intelligence of its own.

The circle in which it stood was another matter entirely. Its lines and daubs, primitive though they might be, exerted a definite opposing force against my valves, and it sent out a darkness that tried to dim the pentacle's brightness and infected the colors with a pinkish-red hue that was almost fiery.

I picked up my small control box and started to modulate the valves, rotating through various pulses and color combinations, searching for one that might defend, and even repel, the red darkness that tried to ooze from the original circle. But in doing so, I almost brought about my own downfall. I discovered that if I used too little blue, or too much red, the strength of the inner circle swelled ever stronger.

It pressed hard against the valves, causing all of them to whine and complain even as I tried to switch to a different modulation. It was as I was attempting to turn up the yellow that I saw the thing that worried me.

The oozing red color thickened inside the original circle, flaring like a raging fire. The demon, no longer quite so static as before, danced in the flame, no longer grinning but screaming soundlessly as if burning in great agony. I felt a blast of heat reach me, even protected as I was by the circles of my electric pentacle. There was also a warm glow on my face, like sun on a hot summer's day, but it was as nothing compared to what appeared to be hungry fires lapping all around the now thrashing red figure that was imprisoned right in the center of all the commotion.

As I increased the power to the yellow valve, more demonic figures in the center circle showed solid form. Indeed, it was soon packed tight with them, a throng, a horde, of cavorting, red figures packed together so tightly that they stood shoulder to shoulder, completely filling the space inside the circle, all screaming as they burned in hellish flame. And even as I had the thought, I knew what I was seeing; I was indeed looking beyond a veil to part of the great beyond I had not previously encountered.

I believe I was being given a vision of Hell itself.

*

Not that I believed in a literal Hell of course, but I knew that old tales, religion and mythology often had their origins in glimpses of compartments or realms of Outer Darkness that the human mind had to try to rationalize to understand them. Perhaps Hell as understood by the wider world was always merely a construct built to make sense of a glimpse of somewhere else, a door through to this burning, red horror I was currently watching.

Wherever it was, the older, inner, circle was still exuding heat and the room was heating up by the second. I was starting to wonder whether the fire that had consumed the cellar ten years before had been intentional at all. I did not have time to dwell on it, for if it got any hotter I was going to have to beat a hasty retreat to avoid ending up in the northern sanitarium alongside the last man to see the same sight.

I pushed the yellow valve to as high a brightness as I dared, and that did seem to bring a momentary coolness wafting through the cellar, but any respite was short lived, and within seconds the red flames lashed harder still against the pentacle. I quickly went through several more permutations of color and modulation as the heat grew almost unbearable and almost cried out in relief when, just as I thought I would have to flee, I set a wave of rapid alternating pulses of blue and yellow washing through the room.

The fires inside the circle dimmed and faded as if doused by water. The demons screamed soundlessly, threw their limbs around in a jerky, almost comical, dance, then they too dimmed and went quiet, leaving only the original, winged beast standing in the center. It looked at me and it appeared to be smiling as it too finally faded and dissipated before disappearing entirely, leaving me alone in a room awash with blue and yellow and a cool, almost chill breeze that came through the wall off the river beyond.

I sat still, watching, for the length of time it took to smoke two cheroots, leaving the pentacle running. The only sound was the hum from my battery and the thin whine that came from the valves as they dimmed and faded. The washes of color splashed across wall, ceiling and floor, but that was the only movement to be seen. There was no reappearance of any demon, dancing or otherwise, in the inner circle.

After my smokes, I lit my oil lamp again and switched off the pentacle, ready to switch it back on at the first sign of any redness or flame. The cellar remained quiet and cool. And I realized something else. It felt empty, and somehow I knew for a fact that I was the only presence here.

I switched on the pentacle again and stepped inside, over both my own circles and into the inner where I scuffed and dragged with my feet until *The Clavicle of Solomon* circle markings were completely erased and scuffed into the ash and dust.

★

I sat there on the steps most of the night. I had the scotch for company now, having taken enough time to fetch it from the bar upstairs, plenty of cheroots left in the case to accompany it, and I had the foresight to have included some dry biscuits and an apple in my kit before leaving Chelsea earlier. I watched the blue and yellow washes of my pentacle play on the walls, felt cool air on my face, and did not see a single sign of the red figure again the whole time.

In the morning, I spent another hour sitting there with the pentacle switched off, to reassure myself that I had indeed been successful. I felt no presence in the room, and there was no sense of any heat, nor sign of any red, flickering, flames.

By the time I packed away my kit and lugged it back upstairs into the bar, I was feeling rather pleased with myself, and ready to go home for a few hours of well-deserved sleep.

It was not to be. I had reached the door to the bar when I met Churchill's man, the carriage driver, on the way in. He had a startled, almost panicked look on his face as he spoke the first words I had heard him utter in our short acquaintance.

"Come quick, Mr. Carnacki. His Lordship is in trouble. He needs you."

★

I sat in the back of the carriage with my box of defenses in my lap as we headed north across the river, clattering at an almost alarming speed over cobbled streets. We sped past several frightened gentlemen on their way to work that had had to dance out of our path to avoid being trampled.

I wondered what Churchill could possibly need me for now. I did not make any connection to the affairs of the night, for I was content in myself that I had quite rid the cellar of any manifestation that had been there. More than that, I was tired and cranky enough to be prepared to tell Churchill what I thought of him to his face should he query my judgement in the matter.

But all such thoughts were blown away when we reached Knightsbridge, the carriage came to a sudden halt, and I was bundled into a tall handsome terraced house and up three flights of stairs to be almost thrown into Churchill's bedchamber.

Churchill sat upright in his bed, still dressed in his nightclothes. He grimaced as if in great pain, rolled his nightshirt sleeve up as high as it would go and held up his right arm as I entered. The palm of his hand was still blackened, as with soot, but the flesh of his arm, all the way up as far as I could see, was red and raw.

It looked for the world as if it had been burned in a great heat.

★

"You cannot tell me that this is a coincidence, Carnacki," Churchill said through gritted teeth after he had dismissed everyone else but myself from the room. I walked over toward the bed and sat in a bedside chair, not wanting to loom over him, and not really knowing what else I could be about.

"It's not me that you need here, man," I said. "It's a bally doctor."

He ignored that, and showed me his blackened palm.

"I got back here last night after a debate in the House,

and saw that I still had the bloody black spot. I scrubbed at it for near an hour with soap, a stiff brush, and several towels. I even thought about taking a bally knife and cutting the skin off when it started to itch like buggery.

"At least a few snifters before I retired to bed managed to take the edge off it and I got some sleep. But in the early hours, I woke, too hot, burning up all over. The bally sweat was lying in a pool under me, and my arm felt like it was on fire."

He showed me the red, inflamed limb again.

"And it's still spreading," he continued, grimacing as fresh pain hit. He had a bottle of scotch at the bedside, and he'd already consumed a third of it since my arrival mere minutes before. He raised it to his lips and took a hefty slug.

"Let me fetch a doctor, man," I said. "This cannot go on."

He grew angry, almost as red in the face as his arm.

"There will be no damned doctors," he replied. "I will not have anyone else seeing me like this. I have a feeling we did this together, Carnacki, you and I. I picked up something from that dashed cellar, caught something off that damned, grinning, red devil. I know that's what it is. And you know it too; do not pretend that is not the case."

I nodded.

"I'm afraid so, old chap," I replied, and spent five minutes quickly relating to him the events of the night, and my, premature as it turned out, thoughts of success.

"Hell?" he said in almost a whisper. "I don't believe in the bally place."

I echoed his words of the day before back at him,

"I don't think it cares, old man," I replied.

★

"So what do we do?" Churchill said after he had digested the information. I saw with some alarm that the red, burning area of skin had spread. I could see it above the collar of his nightshirt; it had started to encroach on his neck.

"It may be that I can replicate what I did with the electric pentacle if we got you back down into the room below the bar," I replied. "But I do not think you are fit to move."

"If Mohammed will not go to the mountain…" he said, with a smile. "Fetch your box of tricks. We'll get it done right here in this room. But keep it as quiet as you can, will you? Can't have any idle chitchat about this spreading among the staff. Their opinion of me is low enough as it is without them thinking I'm some kind of warlock or Satanist."

I left him with the scotch as I went back downstairs to fetch my box of defenses. When I returned, the level in the bottle had dropped considerably, but at least Churchill had some color in his cheeks, and he appeared to be in less pain than before.

"Anything you need from me before you begin, old boy?" he said but I shook my head. I wasn't even sure what I was about to attempt would work, and I did not want to get his hopes up unduly.

I was already clearing an area of floor of rugs. The room was large enough that I had no trouble laying out a full pentacle, chalk first then my valves and wires, with inner and outer circles and plenty of room for a chair inside. That was as well, for I doubted that Churchill would be able to stay on his feet for long. I took the chair from the bedside and placed it on the center of the pentacle, then had to help the man out of bed and across the floor to get him into it.

He felt far too warm to the touch, blasts of heat radiating off him in waves as if he ran a mighty fever. He had brought the scotch bottle with him, and took another hearty swig from the neck after sitting down. There was less than a quarter of the bottle remaining now.

"You had best move bally quickly, Carnacki," he said. "When the scotch is gone, I have a feeling I might be going with it, so whatever it is you are planning, you should do it now, before I slip away completely."

I hooked up the pentacle to the battery, and made sure that the control panel was connected up correctly. My last act was to draw the room's drapes tight and extinguish the lights at the bedside. It was gloomy now in the bedchamber, although not full dark. There was, however, plenty of light to see that Churchill appeared to be sitting inside a fiery red haze that swirled and danced like flame around him.

By this time it was most definitely warmer in the room. Beads of sweat ran from my brow as I finally picked up my small control panel, switched on the pentacle and once again set the yellow and blue valves pulsing in waves in an attempt to beat back the rising, strengthening, influence of the hellish redness.

★

Churchill groaned, then let out a stifled scream as fresh pain wracked his body. Flames cavorted and danced around his bare feet. There was no scorching noticeable on the chair legs, and although he was clearly in a great deal of pain, the pale flesh of his feet and ankles did not burn or char.

He took another long swig of scotch. The pain was etched all across his face, his eyes wet with tears as he looked out at me from within a furious swirl of red fire.

"If there's anything you can do, do it now, for pity's sake, man," he shouted as the flames started to lap higher, covering his whole lower torso.

I pushed the power up to the yellow and blue valves, and set them pulsing faster.

The redness pushed hard against these new waves of color, then, slowly, but definitely, the redness began to retreat. As it did so, the fires solidified, and gained form. A figure stood, bent over Churchill's slumped body. It was the red winged thing again, leathery wings flapping slowly. If it wasn't the same one as I'd seen down in the burned room below the bar, it was its blasted exact double.

The thin, too-red face looked straight at me, and it smiled. It grabbed at Churchill's red, burned arm, and squeezed, hard. Churchill screamed mightily, then slumped, head down on his chest, almost falling out of the chair. I heard someone, one of his men, pound hard on the bedroom door, but I had no time to look that way. I pushed the yellow and blue up to the limit.

The room felt like an oven. My skin tightened on my face as the heat grew, and I tasted burnt flesh in my throat as the demon squeezed and Churchill screamed. At the same instant, the yellow and blue valves both blazed, bright as the sun. A wash of dazzling light fell over Churchill and the chair, a wave that blew the red figure apart and dispersed it into dust and a fine, black, ash that fell and coated the floor at Churchill's feet.

The bedroom door banged open and two of the burly chaps leapt in, ready for action. I do believe they might have felled me there and then had Churchill not raised his head and spoken. His voice was cracked and feeble, but he maintained all of his power of command.

"Leave him be," he said to the two guards. "This man has saved my life."

★

It was only when the guards left the room that I noticed it; all of the burned redness had gone from Churchill's arm. His skin was clear and unmarked, and when he rubbed his right hand flat against his nightshirt, the blackness came off, leaving his palm clean and a dark, greasy streak on the material.

Churchill rose slowly from the chair, and, being careful to avoid both the ash and the circles on the floor, stepped over toward me out of the electric pentacle. He handed me what was left of the scotch bottle.

"You look like a man who could use a drink," he said, and I noted that his voice was strengthening even as he spoke.

I took the scotch gratefully, and drank a long slug of my own.

Churchill walked, almost stumbling, back to his bed and half-sat, half-fell back onto the pillows. He looked tired and wan, but his features were free of pain, and he smiled thinly when he saw my concern.

"I do think I shall live a while longer," he said. And as if to prove it, he leaned over and fetched a cigar and a matchbook from the drawer in his bedside table. He proceeded to light up. He didn't speak again until he was satisfied that he had the log of tobacco leaves well alight. When he eventually looked up at me, he had dark shadows in his eyes, and was all seriousness.

"You saved me, right enough, Carnacki, and I shall not forget that. But nor shall I forget what I saw while sitting there in that dashed circle of yours. Do you know what we did here?

Do you see the import of it?"

"We sent something back to where it should always have been," I replied.

"No," Churchill said softly, shaking his head. "I am not sure that we did. I think all that we did was close a door, not lock one. We almost crossed over a threshold that is always there, always within our reach, a path that is all too easily followed by the unwary and the lost.

"Hell is all too real, Carnacki. I saw it. I opened its doors, had a bally good look around and I felt the heat of the eternal fires of torment. That sight will be with me for the rest of my natural life, however long I am granted on this earth."

★

We spoke only of mundane matters as I cleared up my kit and stowed it in the box, and only returned to the subject right at the last minute as I turned to depart. Churchill was still sitting up in bed, puffing on his cigar, but he looked somewhat lost, almost forlorn.

"You must not speak of this matter to anyone," he said. "Is that understood? I need your promise on that."

"What is there to say? It is over," I said. "That door you spoke of is shut."

Again he smiled wanly.

"In one way, yes, you are probably right. But there is another door, up here, or rather, there is a window here that I cannot help but look through," he said. He tapped at his brow, "I can see it, every time I close my eyes, and I do believe it will always be right in here with me, giving me a glimpse of what awaits at the end of things. I thought yon black dog we encountered on one of our previous meetings was the thing that would haunt me in years to come. But I think this might be even worse."

"Out you go," he said to me, and I left him there with his visions of Hell.

About the Author

William Meikle is a Scottish writer, now living in Canada, with over twenty novels published in the genre press and more than 300 short story credits in thirteen countries. He has books available from a variety of publishers including Dark Regions Press, DarkFuse and Dark Renaissance, and his work has appeared in a large number of professional anthologies and magazines. He lives in Newfoundland with whales, bald eagles and icebergs for company. When he's not writing he drinks beer, plays guitar, and dreams of fortune and glory.

ALSO FROM LOVECRAFT EZINE PRESS

The Endless Fall, by Jeffrey Thomas

Whispers, by Kristin Dearborn

Nightmare's Disciple, by Joseph S. Pulver, Sr.

Autumn Cthulhu, edited by Mike Davis

The Lurking Chronology, by Pete Rawlik

The Sea of Ash, by Scott Thomas

The King in Yellow Tales volume I, by Joseph S. Pulver, Sr.

Blood Will Have Its Season, by Joseph S. Pulver, Sr.

Printed in Great Britain
by Amazon